AFRAID OF THE DARK

Michelle Devlin

AmErica House
Baltimore

First printing

ISBN: 1-58851-298-3
PUBLISHED BY AMERICA HOUSE BOOK PUBLISHERS
www.publishamerica.com
Baltimore

Printed in the United States of America

Take back the pain you gave me
Take back what doesn't belong to me
Take back the shame you gave me
Take back what doesn't belong to me...

...Take back the rage you gave me
Take back the hatred you gave me for me
Take back the anger that nearly killed me
Take back what doesn't belong to me

–Sinead O'Connor

To Terry with love

Acknowledgements

First and foremost I would like to thank God for His inspiration and guidance. I would also like to thank my mother, Kittie Cheney, for her unwavering love and her constant reminders to dream big. I owe a debt of gratitude to Suzette Cheney, Connie Cheney Simecek, and Craig Cheney, my siblings, for their endless encouragement and support during this whole process, and my further thanks to Suzette, Connie, and Kathy Eyerman for being my first proofreaders. I am grateful to my agent, Karen Carr, for taking a chance on me. I am indebted to Ron Mansur and Kathy and Fred Eyerman for their unending faith in me. Thanks also to Sarah Franzenburg, Paul Nuttal, Steph and Mark Pierson, and Heidi and Walt Watzinger, for their continued support. I am grateful to Tina Krumnow, Connie Mendez, Thresa Cerda Roberts, Minerva Thomas, Mamta Chhabra, Phyllis and Elizabeth, without whose love and support I wouldn't be where I am today. I also owe a special thanks to Dr. John E. Marcellus, Don Hlavinka, and Dr. Steven DeAlmeida for helping to put me back together again. And, lastly, thanks to my husband, Terry, for staying with me through my bouts of craziness and my moments of sanity.

Chapter 1

The same disturbing thoughts bounced around my brain for the hundredth time as I drove up the circular parking garage on my way to see Mr. Bradshaw. Why was I doing this? Sure, I had a few idiosyncrasies, but who didn't? It was true that I was afraid of the dark and the nightmares had been occurring more frequently, but it wasn't like I was totally whacko or anything. A therapist seemed a bit extreme for someone who was simply a bit fearful and didn't sleep well.

I circled up and up, looking for a space, eventually following a middle aged woman slouching toward her car. Poor woman. Looks like she's the one in need of counseling. Looks like the perfect victim. Where in the world was she parked?

And what was I doing here? I had a great husband, wonderful friends, good posture. No real problems. The perfect life. I should just turn around and go home before I set this charade into motion. But I didn't. I'd promised Alex I'd go through with at least one visit to the therapist. "Just to see," I said. See what, though, I wasn't sure.

I pulled into the space the woman pulled out of, grabbed my keys and purse, locked the car doors and headed for the elevator. I looked left and right as I walked briskly down the center of the garage, careful not to get too close to a car where a madman may be hiding. When I approached a support pillar I braced myself, trying to think of some sort of self defense technique in case I was grabbed from the other side. What were those female cops on television always doing? I made a mental note to develop a fear inducing stance in case I was confronted one day by a crazy person lurking in a dark corner.

The thumping of the cars driving overhead gave me the willies. It sounded like the whole garage was shaking; that the floor above might cave in at any moment, trapping me in concrete. I made it to the elevator without incident, but now I had to make the decision whether to ride down in the enclosed box or take the stairs. It didn't take a mental giant to know that a garage stairwell was the perfect prowling place for a man to lie in wait. I also had a fear of elevators, though, and especially distrusted garage elevators. Years ago I'd created a safety scale by which to measure elevators; giving hospitals the best rating and parking garages the worst.

I looked at the six people waiting. There were two women, each about fifty, and one man, about seventy years old, standing with an elderly woman I assumed to be his wife. He looked harmless enough. Another woman who looked to be about forty stood next to a boy, about eighteen. Her son? Eighteen was a bad age; raging hormones and all that. But if he was with his mother maybe he wouldn't be a threat. I finally decided I could survive the short ride down if I was in the company of other women. At least if I got stuck I wouldn't be alone with the man and the boy. As I stood with the others in silent vigil I recalled the nightmare I'd had again last night as so many nights before and wondered, as always, how to shake the anxiety that lingered.

The bell signaling the arrival of the elevator drew me from my reverie. The doors parted. Waiting to make sure I would be the last on, therefore first off, I walked into the elevator. I counted in my head – one-one thousand, two-one thousand, three-one thousand – as the doors closed. At the third floor I stepped aside gingerly, allowing the elderly couple to disembark, hoping my movement wouldn't upset the fine balance of weight and counter-weight, and that the elevator wouldn't suddenly go crashing to the basement or, worse yet, refuse to move at all. Finally, the descent began again. And again I counted in my head – one-one thousand, two-one thousand, and so on. With a jolt that only the hyper-vigilant could detect, we landed. I held my breath for the nano-second it took for the doors to part, stepped outside, and breathed a sigh of relief. I'd made it.

It was almost comical, I thought, now that I was safe. I'd been happy the therapist was on the first floor so I wouldn't have to ride the elevator, never once considering the possibility that I may not be able to park on the first floor. I began to worry now about the return trip to my car.

Maybe Alex was right. Maybe it wouldn't hurt for me to see a therapist. This guy was supposed to be good. Alex had heard of him through someone at work. A friend of a friend kind of thing. He'd probably discover I'd been traumatized as a child at some Halloween haunted house and that'd be that.

10

I found the office easily enough and stepped into a surprisingly large room with warm, cozy colors covering the walls. Cool pastel chairs were overstuffed and begging to be sat on. I exhaled audibly.

"May I help you?" the receptionist asked from behind an open window where she could work and spy on the crazies at the same time.

"Yes, hi. I'm Ali Connery. I have a 10:00 appointment with Eric Bradshaw."

"Is this your first visit?"

"Yes, ma'am."

She handed me a clipboard with a single sheet of paper. "Please fill out the front and back. Do you have your insurance card?"

"Yes, hold on." I fumbled through my wallet. "Here you go."

I sat down in a violet chair; my favorite color.

Okay, let's see here. Name, *Ali Connery*. Age, *29. Married, no children*. Address, home phone, occupation, employer, work phone. Blah, blah, blah. Blah, blah, blah. Were whole forests being felled to produce the same form for thousands of doctors throughout North America? Was there one desperate person whose sole job in the universe was to sit in a cubicle in some obscure city and mail out 'the form?'

Reason for visit? Hmmm. That was a good one. Lack of resistance to my husband's insistence? Afraid of the dark? Just plain tired of being afraid all the time? Nightmares? Where to begin? Restlessness – that sounded good. Not too desperate. Don't want to put him off right away.

I finished the form and handed it to the receptionist in exchange for my insurance card. I sat back down in the violet chair and glanced at my watch, 9:45 a.m. I wonder if this guy's on time. Did the receptionist tell him I was already there, an early bird, eliciting a mark in my permanent record before I even walked into his office? What did that say about me? Come to think of it, what did my handwriting say about me? Was he going to scrutinize it before he saw me, seeing that I printed instead of wrote? Had I not grown into a mature woman? Was I trying to hide in some child's world?

I opened the book I'd brought with me, *Sacajewa*. I'd only read a hundred pages and hadn't fully committed to it. I'd enjoyed what

I'd read, but was still at the "let's see how this goes" stage. I read the same paragraph twice and closed the book. No point in pretending I could concentrate. I glanced at the magazines. A current copy of *Photography*. I turned the pages, studying each photograph; the subject, the expressions, the framing, the lighting. I really should get my camera out and go out for a day of picture taking soon.

I looked at my watch, 9:55. Was he going to make me wait? See how I handled it? 10:05. I realized I was tapping my foot. Was this some sort of test? I set the magazine down and sat perfectly still. 10:10. The inner door opened.

"Mrs. Connery?"

"Yes, hi." I stood up.

"Hello. I'm Eric Bradshaw. Come on in."

He was good looking. Tall, mid-fifties. The proverbial graying temples, the proverbial pearly whites, and neat as the proverbial pin.

I followed him a short way to his office. He stopped and gestured for me to enter first. His office was a flip of the outer office, cool pastel walls with warm, cozy furniture.

He closed the door behind us. "Take a seat."

"Where?"

"Wherever you'd be most comfortable."

I looked around his office. A black leather chair was pushed up to a desk that held papers, magazines, and a picture of his family, presumably. Across from a ceiling high bookshelf, filled to capacity, were about a dozen framed documents. I was curious about them, but too timid to walk over, not wanting him to think I was checking up on him.

"Where do you sit?" I asked. "Oh, I guess wherever I don't sit, huh?" Great. Already I sounded like an idiot and we hadn't even started yet. Or had we? Was this another test? Was he making mental notes to jot down the second I left? *Couldn't even make a simple decision as to where to sit.* I sat in the nearest chair, deciding the couch was too cliché. He sat in a chair catty-cornered to my left, close but not so close that he was invading my space. Very good.

"Do you prefer being called Mrs. Connery or Ali?"

"Ali."

"Fine. We'll go into detail later about what's going on with you, but if you could sum up in just one sentence why you're here today, what would that be?"

"Oh... Well... Hmmm... I guess... Uh..."

"Take your time."

Oh, God. Now I sounded like a blithering idiot. Another note. *Can't form complete sentences.*

"Well, um, I guess I'd say because I feel on the verge of throwing up all the time."

"Okay."

Did I hear a chuckle? No, more of an audible grin.

"That's fine. Why do you think you feel that way?" he asked.

"I don't know. I'm just nervous and afraid a lot."

"Afraid of what?"

"Well, I'm afraid of the dark. Afraid I'm going to be raped, mugged, and murdered at every turn. Afraid someone's going to break into our house and kill me. I have locks on all my windows and three locks on my front door." I began to feel anxious. Maybe I was sounding a bit too paranoid. Better watch that. He'd have me in a loony bin in no time with more locks than I wanted.

"How long have you been this afraid?"

"As long as I can remember. I just can't seem to get over it. It's like I never grew up."

"Why do you think you're so afraid? Have you ever been the victim of a crime? Robbed or mugged?"

"Yes, actually, I have. Been robbed, I mean. It was five years ago. I worked as a cashier at a credit union and we were robbed. Made us lie on the floor and everything. Then made us go into the ladies room. I thought that's when they were going to kill us and I kept thinking 'Mama and Alex are going to be upset if I get killed at work today.' Alex is my husband. Anyway, it just confirmed all the fears I've had all my life. Someone's out to get me."

"I see."

I started crying then. Not tears gently sliding down my cheeks in a ladylike, damsel in distress manner. No. Crying, sobbing, boohooing.

He stood up and walked to his desk, probably to press a secret button to alert the receptionist to break out the committal forms; they had a live one. In a moment, though, he turned back to me with a box of tissues in his hand.

"Thank you. I'm sorry. I really don't know what's wrong with me. I seem to be doing that a lot lately."

"Did you have any type of counseling after the robbery?"

"No. And I was terrified to go back to work. I didn't go in the next day, but after that I did. I was so scared I jumped every time the little bell went off when someone walked in the door. I quit three months later. I was a wreck."

"I'd say you're suffering from Post Traumatic Stress Syndrome from the robbery. Are you familiar with that?"

"Yes."

"Well, we can deal with that, but we want to find out why you were so afraid before that incident. Is there anything before the robbery that might have caused you to feel frightened? More frightened than the usual childhood fears?"

"I don't know, maybe..." I hesitated. "Well, yeah, there is, but I can't talk about that right now." I spoke while I dabbed at my tears. "I keep having the same nightmares, too. There are two in particular that I have off and on."

"Can you tell me about them?"

"Well, in the first one I'm locked in a small room and it's dark. At one point I'm banging on the door and hollering for someone to let me out. Then when the door finally opens I cower back into the corner. A male figure walks in, but I can't make out his age or his features because the light from the open door blinds me, putting him in silhouette. All I know for sure is that he's male and that he's there to hurt me. I don't know how I know that, I just do. Anyway, he walks up to me and just as he bends and reaches out for me I wake up, terrified. Sometimes I wake Alex up and ask him to put his arm around me and hold me."

"What about the other dream?"

"It's really weird. In that one I'm standing on a stage, like at a school auditorium. You know like if you were in a spelling bee or something. Anyway, the auditorium is filled with people and I'm standing at the microphone. Oh, God, this is really embarrassing."

"It's okay. Go on."

"Well, I'm standing there in front of everyone with nothing on but my bra and panties and instead of spelling words, you know, well, I have to tell them all the bad things I've done in my life. Like I'm reciting some list to them while they gasp and boo. Pretty weird, huh?"

"No, not really. Any others?"

"I dream a lot about someone trying to hurt me, but those are the two nightmares I have on a regular basis. Oh yeah, wait. I also have a recurring dream that's pretty neat. I really like it. I dream sometimes that I can fly! It's wonderful. The main part of that dream is that I have to believe. I mean truly believe that I can fly, and then I can! Kind of like Peter Pan, I guess. So I do it. I fly above everything; soar through the sky looking below me and feeling like I have all this power to just go where I want and see what I want; that I'm in total control. I love that dream. In fact, sometimes when I go to bed, I concentrate real hard and try to dream that one. But I'm not very successful."

"That sounds like fun."

"Yeah, it is. I love it."

"Tell me more about growing up in your family. What are some of the things that scared you when you were younger?"

And so I sat there telling stories, recalling all the times I was afraid growing up. How my father was a merchant marine and gone months at a time and how every time there was an alarming noise in the backyard my mother went out by herself to investigate, and how I was scared for her. Scared she was going to get hurt and scared we four kids were going to be left all alone. And angry. Angry there wasn't a man in the house to protect us.

How I was home alone with my girlfriend one rainy night when a drunken man started beating on our door, demanding we let him in. How Pam and I tried to pretend we weren't alone, that my dad was home, only to discover a few minutes later, when Mama returned, that he was some cousin from out of town who'd chosen that night to surprise us with a visit.

How my brother and sisters used to jump out of closets in the hallway as I headed for bed at night, just to hear me scream.

How they made up stories of an escaped asylum patient who

15

spent the evenings prowling the neighborhood looking for young girls to rip apart with his hook.

And on and on and on.

Maybe a second visit wouldn't hurt.

Chapter 2

"So how it'd go today?" Alex asked.

"Good, I think."

"Did you like him?"

"Yeah, I did." I set the placemats on the table, then reached in the drawer for knives and forks. "It seemed like he really cared about me. I couldn't believe it, but I hadn't been there ten minutes and I was crying. I felt like an idiot."

"Well, I'm sure he's quite used to that. To people crying, I mean."

Alex was a therapist himself and had seen his share of tears.

"Do you want wine?" he asked.

"Yes, and lots of it. I'm exhausted."

"Therapy has that effect. Would you hand me the corkscrew please?"

I handed him the corkscrew, then grabbed two wine glasses while he opened the bottle of Chardonnay. We sat down to our Greek salads and wine.

"So," Alex asked, "Do you want to talk about it?"

"Well, there's really not much to tell."

"What did you discuss? Or would you rather not say?"

"No, it's not that." I pushed the olives around on my plate. "I don't know. It seems kind of strange looking back on it. I mean, well, one minute he was asking me why I was there and the next minute I was crying. But I don't feel like I really told him anything. You know what I mean?"

"Yes, actually, I do."

"He just seemed to know what to say to stir things up."

"He sounds good. That doesn't usually happen on a first visit."

"Yeah, well, I was pretty anxious by the time he called me in." I looked up at him. "Oh, I forgot. He thinks I'm suffering from Post Traumatic Stress Syndrome."

"That doesn't surprise me. I've mentioned that." Alex poured more wine into my glass. "Did he say he thinks he can help you?"

"Yes, but he said it's obviously my decision whether to see him

17

again or not. He also said he'd like to talk some more about my nightmares, get more into them; why I keep dreaming someone's trying to hurt me. Why do you think he said that? You think the dreams are really important? You think he thinks so?"

"I think you should ask him. It wouldn't be right for me to offer an opinion. Want more wine?"

"No, I guess not. I'll just end up with a headache." He poured the remainder of the wine into his glass. "I just wish I wasn't so scared all the time," I said quietly, not really speaking to Alex, but to myself.

"You going to see him again?" He didn't look up at me, but I heard the anxiety in his voice. The "Please say yes." The "Please tell me you're going to finally do something about this." The "Please, I can't live with such a paranoid nut job any longer."

"Yes, I am. I figure it can't hurt." I stared at my plate, trying to get lost in the pattern of tiny flowers. "I have an appointment for next week."

Did I hear a sigh of relief?

"I almost forgot. He wants me to take some kind of test, too."

"Which one?"

"I don't know. He said it was long, about 500 questions."

"Must be the MMPI." He leaned back in his chair. "How do you feel about that?"

I knew that tone. It was his therapist voice and I had the sudden urge to remind him I was his wife. He did that sometimes, forgot who I was and started talking to me like I was a client. It usually drove me crazy, but tonight, for some reason, it had a comforting effect. He used hypnotherapy with a few clients and he had the perfect voice for it – soft, soothing, reassuring. I stared at him while he talked. He was six-one, a gentle, kind man with fair skin, the gift of a Scandinavian heritage. Soft blond hair swept across his forehead, and, I hate to admit it, I was a bit jealous of his high cheekbones. He had a perfectly straight nose and pencil thin lips. I could never decide if his eyes, the color of cold blue gems, or the incredibly sexy dimple on his left cheek was my favorite feature. My opinion changed as often as the sun rose. I was grateful he continued to put up with me and my array of idiosyncrasies; few men would.

18

"Sweetheart?"

"What?"

"I asked how you felt about that?"

"Oh. Fine, I guess. At least I'll take a look at it."

"That sounds like a good plan." He stood up and started clearing the table. "You through with your salad?"

"I guess so." I grabbed both wine glasses with one hand, the empty wine bottle with the other, and followed him into the kitchen.

"He said if I wanted to drop by the office in the next day or two I could pick up the test, then get it back to him before my next visit. Said he had an idea of where to begin with me, but that he'd like to have it confirmed, make sure we weren't spending time going in the wrong direction."

"Makes sense."

"His office is pretty close to yours. Do you think you could pick it up for me? I'd really appreciate it. Now that I've set this in motion, I'm anxious to move forward. I don't want to waste any time. You know how I am."

"No, huh-uh. How are you?"

"Cute, real cute. Would you mind?"

"Of course not. I'll drop by tomorrow during lunch."

"Thanks darling, I really appreciate it."

He grinned. "No problem. I'll just add it to your tab."

I tossed and turned while Alex snored next to me. He was amazing. He could go from awake to asleep in less time than it took me to arrange my pillow. He'd tried to teach me his secret; a kind of self hypnosis thing, but I'd never been able to master it. Didn't really have the patience to practice it enough for it to be effective. I watched him jealously as I tossed and turned, my thoughts racing. Why had I been so emotional today in Mr. Bradshaw's office? What had happened that set me off? What had he said? I stared at the clock radio, 2:10 a.m. This was ridiculous. I got up and fixed myself a good strong vodka with 7-Up and logged onto the Internet. Maybe a little browsing for first editions would distract me.

I finally went back to bed about 4:30 a.m. after five drinks. Alex stirred, slipping his arm around me as I snuggled up next to him, as close as I possibly could without actually lying underneath him. I was asleep instantly.

The next morning I woke up tired and dragging with a hangover to add to my list of miseries. I was in the kitchen slapping strawberry jam on a piece of toast when Alex walked in.

"Good morning, sweetheart." He gave me a kiss. "How are you this morning?"

"Hi, okay," I yawned. "But I had a nightmare last night and even though I can't remember what it was about, I feel spooked. I can't seem to shake it."

"Yeah, I know. Remember? I woke you up."

"What? No. You're kidding."

"You don't remember? Really?"

"No."

"You were making a strange high pitched whine, like a cat being tortured. And you almost killed me with your hands. Acted like you were trying to chop my head off."

"Oh, that's right. I thought I was being attacked by some crazy man in the garage at Mr. Bradshaw's office. I was defending myself."

"Well I hope it never happens. I think you'd only succeed in scaring the hell out of them with that yell. What was that?"

"Oh," I answered, embarrassed now. "It must've been my karate yell."

"I think you've seen too many movies." He gave me a kiss on the cheek as he reached across me for the bread.

The lingering effects of the nightmare remained with me the rest of the day. I was tired and anxious. Fortunately I didn't have much work to do. I'd talked to the office and they didn't need the data entry completed until the end of the week. I worked about three hours, then took a nap. Working from home had its advantages.

When I woke up I still didn't feel rested. As I struggled through cleaning the kitchen, vacuuming and dusting, I thought of my visit with Mr. Bradshaw and how easily I'd collapsed into tears. It all seemed a bit surreal to me in hindsight.

That night Alex brought home the test Mr. Bradshaw wanted me to take. I glanced through it before we ate supper. He wasn't joking;

it was more than 500 questions. How could anyone even think of 500 questions to ask another human being. I couldn't even play Twenty Questions because I always ran out of ideas after, "Is the person a male? Is he alive? Is he an artist?" I hate that game.

I put the test aside for later. Alex told me about his day as we worked in the kitchen making chef salads. We both needed to lose weight so we were on our salad kick. It was always a bit weird listening to him talk about work because of the confidentiality issue. He spoke in generalities and referred to clients by fictitious names that we made up. We talked about Bob and Betty and Sandra in very broad terms while chopping and slicing.

After supper I went into my office behind closed doors so I could give my full attention to the test. I was anxious to complete it and get it back to Mr. Bradshaw before my next appointment.

Okay, let's see here. I was supposed to read each statement and decide whether it was "true as applied to me" or "false as applied to me." Seemed simple enough.

Number one--*I like mechanics magazines*. Well, sure, I guess. I mean, I like to see how things work. But would I really like a whole magazine about it? Don't know. Better come back to that one.

Number two--*I have a good appetite*. Definitely true. All I had to do was look in the mirror for that answer. I needed to lose ten pounds.

Number three--*I wake up fresh and restored most mornings*. True. Oops, no, that'd be false. Actually, it'd be sometimes. What if it's 50/50? Better come back to that one.

Number four--*I think I would like the work of a librarian*. That's a no-brainer. Of course I would. I love books; love being around them. Oh, but I wouldn't want to have to do all that reference work they do and I wouldn't want to have to be quiet all the time. So I guess I'd like some of it. Dang it. There wasn't a place for "some of it." True or false? I guess I'd go with True. I mean nobody likes every part of their job, right? Okay good. Two down.

Fifteen minutes later I'd skipped thirty questions and answered only eight. This was going to take longer than I thought. Maybe I should go with my first instinct and not think so much about each question. I was analyzing them to death.

Number 39--*My sleep is fitful and disturbed*. Well my gosh, they just asked me if I woke up fresh and restored. How would it look if I said yes to both? I'd better see how I answered the other one.

Three hours later I finished the test and sealed it in the envelope provided. I began immediately to worry about the results. Maybe I'd given some wrong answers. Maybe I hadn't thought about some of the questions fully. Maybe it'd confirm the fact that I was a full blown, whacked-out, obsessive compulsive, paranoid, anal retentive nut! But surely Alex would've mentioned that to me by now.

Another night of tossing and turning. Another night of vodka and the Internet.

Chapter 3

The week flew by. Alex had dropped off my completed test at Mr. Bradshaw's office and I sat once again in the violet chair in the waiting room. At least there weren't any men in white coats waiting for me when I walked in. That was a good sign. Maybe they were waiting in Mr. Bradshaw's office; not wanting to make a scene in front of the other woman waiting. She looked normal enough. Wonder what she was there for. Was she a whacked-out, obsessive compulsive, paranoid, anal retentive nut also? And why was she waiting there? Did she have an appointment with one of the other therapists or had I confused the time of my appointment? How could we both have the same appointment time? It wasn't like a regular doctor's office where they dashed in and out like mice looking for bits of cheese. Was he going to cut my time short? I couldn't feel relaxed talking to him if I knew someone else was waiting. It'd be rather like someone looking over your shoulder while you work. Or maybe she was ahead of me. That would mean I'd really screwed up on the time or he was running very late and I'd have to sit there for an hour. I wouldn't want her to cut her session short on my account. I gave her a friendly, hi, how are you, I'm not really crazy smile and went back to the photography magazine. I hadn't even bothered to bring a book this time. Not into the office that is. I had one in the car. One never knew when one might get stuck waiting for a train to pass or have car trouble and have to sit and wait for help or any number of potential time consuming, time wasting activities. Times when one had the opportunity to read, even if it was only one sentence.

The door to the inner office opened. I immediately became tense, straightening my shoulders and smiling the type of fake smile usually seen on a toothpaste billboard. I wouldn't be caught off guard. The woman I shared the waiting room with stood up. A boy about twelve years old walked toward her. She gave me a polite nod, smiled at the receptionist and they left.

About ten minutes later the door opened and Eric greeted me. I'd made the decision the night before to call him Eric. I didn't feel like

I could talk confidentially to a man I referred to as mister.

We walked down the hall toward his office. "How you doing today Ali?"

Was that a trick question? Was he being polite or did he really want to know how I was? Had the session already started or was that merely a formality until we got behind closed doors?

"Fine, thanks," I finally answered, deciding to go the polite route. "How are you?"

"I'm doing well, thanks. Glad to be inside in the air conditioning."

Aha, it was just polite chatter. "Yeah, I know what you mean. It's already getting bad out there. Makes me dread the oncoming summer." Uh-oh, now I sounded like a whiner.

We reached his office and I sat in the same chair as before. A creature of habit? Should I have switched to a different chair this time? Was I predictable?

"So, how's your week been?"

"Fine, just fine. Everything's fine." Oh crap. There I go. More notes in the permanent record. *Constantly repeats herself.* "How are you?" I asked.

"I'm doing great," he answered, politely ignoring the fact that he'd answered that same question only thirty seconds earlier and was obviously dealing with someone who exhibited signs of short term memory loss. "I have the results from the test you took and I'd like to go over them with you."

"Sure, okay." My heart raced. Here it comes.

"There weren't really any surprises. It pretty well confirmed what I thought after our first meeting. Do you find that you have mood swings?"

"Well, yeah, I guess."

"Periods of severe highs and lows?"

"I do get extremely depressed sometimes. Have fits of crying. Feel like there's no reason to live. I want everyone to just leave me alone."

"What about highs?"

"Oh yeah. I get crazy! I'm like a mad woman!" Oops, better watch my choice of words. "I mean I get in moods where my mind's going faster than I can keep up. I'll be doing three things at once while I'm wondering what I should do next. And I don't sleep much. I'm just constantly going."

"I see."

"I don't seem to be able to live in the moment when I'm in my... uh, wound-up phase." Ooh, I liked that, sounded much better than crazy or mad woman.

He looked backed down at the sheaf of papers with my test results. It was weird to think this was only the second time I'd met the man and already he knew more about me than some of my long-time friends. Were all my deep dark secrets laid bare on pieces of 8-1/2x11 snow white paper? Did he already know the strange thoughts that flitted through my mind on occasion? Maybe I wouldn't have to say anything more. Maybe he could just read my results and fix me. Kind of like an EKG – the results show, Mrs. Connery, that you should exercise more, watch your cholesterol, and take a Valium every morning.

I looked up to see Eric staring at me. Had he said something and I missed it? *Short attention span.* "I'm sorry, did you ask me a question?"

"No, you were talking about living in the moment."

"Oh, yeah. Well, for example, while Alex and I are on the way to the movies, I'll ask him what he wants to do after the movie. I'm always looking for what's next."

"Why do you think you do that?"

"I don't know. I just have this need, uh, desire, I mean, to have things planned out. I don't like to be idle." That sounded good. Idle was a nice mature sounding word.

"I see. Why do you think that is?"

Now I was getting annoyed. Why was he asking me all these questions? He was supposed to be the expert, not me. That's why I was there; for him to tell me why I was a crazy lady. Not for me to try to explain it to him. I smiled at him. "I get bored kind of easily. Like to stay busy."

"Okay, fine." He wrote something down. "You like to read, don't you?"

"Oh yeah. I love books. Always have. In fact, I collect first editions. It's really fun. Kind of like being on a scavenger hunt all the time. It's the one thing I do where I can enjoy the moment; that I don't keep thinking about what's next. I relax the second I set foot in a bookstore."

"So you've experimented with drugs in the past?"

Whoa! That came out of left field. Did he do that on purpose? Get me all comfortable talking about my hobby, then pull the rug out from under me? I'd have to stay alert. I wonder if Alex does that to people. It didn't seem fair.

"Ah, well, you know, how it is, sex, drugs, and rock and roll." I gave him what I thought was my conspiratorial grin. "It's not a big deal, really, but I have inhaled."

"Have you ever used anything other than alcohol and Marijuana?"

I straightened up in the chair. Stopped swinging my leg. Where in the test did it show that? The only drug reference was, "I've enjoyed the use of Marijuana," and I answered true. I thought it was a harmless enough question. Maybe I should have lied. Should I lie now?

"Yes," I finally answered.

"What other drugs have you used?"

"Well, it's been awhile."

"Can you remember some of them?"

Oh great. Now he thinks the drugs totally vegged out my memory. "Sure," I answered.

"Would you please tell me what they were?"

"Sure." I put my hands in my lap and looked straight at him. He wasn't going to bully me. I wasn't ashamed of my past behavior. "Acid, Ecstasy, Liquid X, coke, anything I could get my hands on. If it was a pill, I took it. If it was a powder I snorted it."

"Ever do any intravenous drugs?"

"Nope. Stayed away from that. I always wanted to try heroin and even had the opportunity, but didn't because I knew that'd be the final straw with Alex."

"So, drug use is a part of your past. Something you did to fit in; peer pressure?"

"Sure, that sounds good."

26

"When's the last time you smoked Marijuana?"

Damn. Did he have some kind of radar? How did he know what to ask? I lowered my eyes. Maybe he could bully me after all.

I heard him move in his chair. "Ali?"

I looked up. "Well, hmmm. That would be, uh, three days ago."

"I see." More scribbling on his legal pad.

Damnit. Maybe I'd made a mistake in coming here. Maybe I should just slip away quietly and not return. I could excuse myself to go to the ladies room. No, too obvious. Maybe I could start a coughing fit or feign nausea. Tears slipped from my eyes.

"I'd like to help you, Ali, but I need your cooperation. Would you like to continue?"

"Yes," I whispered.

"Good. First I'd like you to see a psychiatrist here at the office."

Oh good. He really did think I was whacko. I started fiddling with the throw pillow on the couch. What had I gotten myself into?

"I'd like you to talk with him and see what he recommends. He may want to put you on anti-depressants while we continue with your therapy. To help regulate your mood swings so they're not so extreme. How do you feel about that?"

"Okay, I guess."

"His name's Ian McCain. He's here in the office so you can make an appointment on your way out. I'll talk to him and let him know to expect you. Do I have your permission to speak with him about you?"

"Yes, sure. I guess."

"See you in two weeks at the same time then?"

I wiped the tears from my cheeks. "Okay, that's good." He handed me a receipt in exchange for the check I handed him, then stood up and opened the door. I had been dismissed.

"Take care of yourself, Ali."

I walked to my car in a bit of a daze. Things seem to be moving along of their own momentum. I felt somewhat out of control of my life all of a sudden.

Chapter 4

I stopped at a bookstore on the way home to regain my inner peace. I was surprised my session with Eric had caused such an unsettling in me. I searched the shelves of used books, looking for a title to add to my collection. I had to work, though, to calm myself; had to actually remind myself to relax. That scared me. I'd never had to do that in a bookstore before. It had always been an immediate effect and now I felt my one sure sanctum had been threatened.

I walked the aisles, breathing deeply and slowly. I sat on the floor thumbing through books. It finally worked. I felt the calm wash over me. Then it happened. I spotted *Oral History* by Lee Smith. One of my favorite books in the world by one of my favorite authors! I picked it up, hesitantly, afraid the dust jacket or book might be damaged. I turned it up and down in my hand looking for the dreaded remainder mark. There was none and the jacket was clean. I opened it to see that no one had written their name in it, nor was it price clipped. The book and pages looked great. I flipped to the copyright page. I couldn't believe it, it was a first. I broke into a grin and let out a quiet "yes!" then looked around to see if anyone might have seen or heard me. How much was it? $5.98. Unbelievable. I held the book close to my chest and closed my eyes.

I couldn't wait to tell Alex about my book find, and, of course, talk to him about my session with Eric. Shortly after I'd finished entering the book in my database, I heard the car in the driveway. I hurried to meet him at the door.

"Hi darling, how are you? How was your day?"

"I'm okay. Had a good day, I guess. Tired."

"Can I fix you a cocktail?" I was nearly jumping out of my skin, wanting to tell him about my book, but wanted him to get settled first.

"That'd be great, thanks."

I headed to the kitchen to grab the rum and Coke from the pantry and picked up the vodka and 7-Up while I was at it. Might as well join him.

Alex was sitting in the big cream colored leather chair in the living room when I walked in with our drinks.

"I'm really anxious to hear about your day, hon, but first I have to tell you what I found. You won't believe it. Wait, no. Let me show you." I scampered into my office and back into the living room, clutching the book. "Look! Look what I found!" I held it out to him.

He took the book from me. "A first? Oh, sweetheart, that's wonderful. Where'd you get it?"

"Half Price books on Elkins."

"You must have really been excited to find it. I know how you love Lee Smith."

"Yeah, I couldn't believe it. I wanted to keep looking for more books, but I was so nervous and excited I just wanted to get home with it. Isn't that goofy? What a great day. Now, tell me about yours."

I settled on the couch and drank my vodka while we talked.

"You want to eat soon?" I asked. "Or wait awhile?"

"Let's have one more drink. I'll be ready to eat about 7:00 or 7:30. Is that alright?"

"Sure, I'll fix us another one."

"Do you have anything in mind for supper?" he hollered into the kitchen.

"Yeah, thought I'd fix some linguine with prosciutto, and tomatoes and mozzarella for a salad." I walked back to the living room with our drinks. "That okay?"

"Yeah, sounds great. Do you mind if I don't help tonight? I'm really tired."

"No, of course not. I feel great. Besides, I didn't work at all today. I'll finish my drink and get started while you relax."

"How'd your visit with Eric go today?" Alex asked over dinner. "Did he have your test results?"

"Yeah. It was interesting, I guess. And kind of weird."

"How so?"

"It was just strange that all of a sudden he knew so much about me, about my personality. He asked about my mood swings. Said he wants me to see a psychiatrist. A Dr. Ian McCain. You ever heard of him?"

"No, I haven't."

"Eric thinks Dr. McCain may want to put me on anti-depressants to help even out my highs and lows a bit. What do you think?"

"It doesn't matter what I think. What do you think about it?"

Oh great. He was in therapist mode. "Alex, don't do that. I need to know what you think – as my husband."

"If it would help, maybe you should give it a try. It's up to you, of course. Why don't you just wait till you see Dr. McCain and take it from there?"

"Good idea. My appointment's for next week. You want some strawberries for dessert? Or we have watermelon."

"Nothing now. Maybe some watermelon later. I think I'd just like to watch some television. Anything good on tonight?"

"Law and Order comes on in half an hour."

"Perfect. I'll watch that, then go to bed. I'm glad tomorrow's Friday."

Alex assumed his position in the leather chair while I knitted. I was making a baby blanket for friends in Dublin. *Law and Order* was one of my favorite shows, but I had trouble concentrating on it. I also had trouble keeping track of where I was in my knitting. I waited for the commercials, then set my needles down. "Alex, do you think I should continue with this?"

He pressed the mute button on the remote. "With what, sweetheart? The baby blanket? Of course. Why wouldn't you?"

"No, I mean therapy." I laughed. "I don't know why you can't read my mind."

"Yeah, I need to work on that."

"Seriously, what do you think?"

"I think you should do whatever you want."

"Dang it, Alex. Give me a straight answer. What do you think?"

He sighed. "I think therapy could be very beneficial. You've struggled with your fears and nightmares for years and I'd be happy if you could find some resolution. I'd like to see you happy. I think you should certainly give it a try. See what happens. But, Ali, it's ultimately your decision. You're the only one who can say for sure if it's being helpful or even if you want to deal with it."

"Deal with what?" The commercials had ended, but I didn't want to end the conversation. "What do I have to deal with?"

31

"Well, what's kept you frightened all these years. Finally face the underlying cause of all your fears."

"Oh, yeah." I picked up my knitting. He pressed the mute button again and continued to watch the program.

When the show ended he stood up. "You coming to bed now?"

"No. I don't think I could sleep. I've got so much stuff running around in my brain, I can't seem to stop it. You go on. I think I'll have another drink and work on my book database. I can't seem to get into my knitting. I need more of a distraction."

"Okay." He gave me a kiss goodnight.

"Oh, honey, I almost forgot. Eric put a code on my receipt for a diagnosis. I guess for the insurance company. Will you look it up in the DSM tomorrow? I want to know what he's thinking."

Chapter 5

The week dragged by with me obsessing about what Alex had said about the underlying cause of my fears, and about my upcoming appointment with Dr. McCain. I didn't have any idea what to expect and kept running potential scenarios through my mind. One had Dr. McCain telling me to stop being so self-involved and to stop wasting his time and Eric's with my petty problems. Another had him flipping through his diagnostic manual, fingers flying across the pages, looking for a label appropriate to my particular brand of idiosyncratic behavior. And still another had him laughing uproariously every time I completed a sentence, then responding with, "You think you have problems, listen to this."

By the time I actually went to the office for my appointment, I was a basket case. How much did he already know about me? Had Eric told him about the drugs? Had he seen the results of my MMPI test?

Once again I found myself tapping my foot as I sat in my violet chair in the waiting room. I didn't even try to concentrate on the photography magazine. I considered thumbing through the *Reader's Digest* to read the jokes, but didn't. I decided it might seem a bit strange to the spying receptionist if I sat in a room by myself laughing. So I just sat, letting my mind bounce from one thought to another like a Mexican jumping bean.

Finally a man of about sixty opened the door and invited me in. He looked to be just over six feet tall, broad shouldered with a barrel chest. He had thick gray hair that was so curly I wondered how he ever got a comb through it. He could stand to lose twenty pounds, but who was I to talk?

"Ali?"

"Yes, hi," I answered, walking toward him.

"Hello, I'm Ian McCain." He didn't refer to himself as Doctor. I liked that. I once knew someone with a Ph.D. in geography. He was so pretentious he had his wife introduce him as Dr. Evans. Made me want to puke. "My office is just at the end of the hall."

When we reached his office he stopped and gestured for me to go ahead of him. I walked into a large room filled with bright, vibrant yellows, blues, reds, and greens. A corner of the room held an array of dolls, puzzles, paper and crayons. In another corner stood a punching bag. Interesting. Hope he didn't think I was going to get into any of that weird, hit the punching bag, get rid of your anger crap. For one thing I didn't have any anger to get rid of. Secondly, I was way too self-conscious to display any emotion in such a nonverbal manner.

I sat in the nearest chair, a comfortable blue and yellow wingback. He sat in a nice leather chair with an ottoman, about six feet directly across from me. Different approach from Eric. Not quite so intimate. More of a "you can confide in me, but I'm the one in charge here." A box of tissues sat on the coffee table between us.

"So, Ali, how are you feeling today?"

"Fine, thank you." Oh great, here I go again. If I was so fine, then what was I doing sitting in a psychiatrist's office in the middle of a Thursday afternoon? Why wasn't I off enjoying my fine life?

"Can you tell me what you're feeling right now?"

"A bit anxious. You know, not knowing quite what to expect."

"That's natural. What else?"

"Nervous."

"Why is that do you think?"

"I don't know. I've been feeling like that a lot lately. Like I can't sit still, feel like I'm going to jump out of my skin." I fought the urge to bounce out of the chair and start pacing the floor. Didn't want to appear too wigged out on my first visit.

"Is that all?"

"No, sometimes I feel just the opposite. All I want to do is lie on the floor with my headphones on and listen to music; not answer the phone or talk to anyone."

"Are you having trouble sleeping?"

"Yes, it's terrible. For some reason I really dread going to bed at night. I stay up till all hours, having a few drinks, trying to relax enough to go to bed. When I finally do I toss and turn for at least an hour, usually longer. I sleep about four or five hours, then wake up raring to go. It's exhausting, but I get a lot done." I smiled at him. "I call it my crazy phase." Whoops, really must watch my vocabulary.

"And when you're not in that phase?"

"Then I don't want to do anything, not communicate, not answer the phone, not read emails, not go out. Just wish everyone would leave me the hell alone. Oh, sorry."

"That's okay."

"I call that my crash and burn phase."

He chuckled. "I like the names you've chosen. I see you've got two older sisters and an older brother."

"Yes, that's right."

"What was it like growing up in your family?"

"It was okay. Nothing strange. Not much different from everyone else's childhood, I guess. My mom and dad divorced when I was seven. My dad was an alcoholic and my mom finally just got fed up with him. She remarried when I was nine. My father was a merchant marine. He'd be out of the country for two to three months, then home for two to three months. I remember when he'd arrive home it was like Christmas. He had all sorts of gifts for us from all around the world." Oh great. Now I was rambling.

"I see. That must've been fun."

"Yeah, when there was a school play, they always came to me for props. You know, like wooden shoes, or conical hats, or a sari. It was pretty neat. Made me feel important." I couldn't seem to shut up. "We had dolls from all around the world, but my girlfriend and I ruined them by playing with them. We were really too young to appreciate them."

"So, your mother's married to your step-father."

"Oh, no. Sorry. She divorced him and remarried my father when I was nineteen. That's a long story. But he told her he'd quit drinking and I guess she believed him. It wasn't true and she re-divorced him years later."

"Have you ever tried to hurt yourself?"

Oh my gosh, he really did think I was whacko. Can't get lulled into thinking we were just having a friendly chat here.

"No, not really. I did use to bang my fist against the wall. Oh yeah, I used to scratch and tear at my arms also."

"Thoughts of hurting anyone else?"

"Oh, heavens no. I apologize to a dog if I accidentally bump him.

35

I couldn't ever hurt anyone."

"Had thoughts of suicide?"

"Well, occasionally. Like, you know, sometimes when I'm driving I wonder what it'd be like just to step on the gas and keep going as fast as I could – straight off the freeway. Or taking a bunch of pills when I'm drinking. Just lie down and go to sleep. But I wouldn't really go through with it. I wouldn't do that to Alex or my family."

"Do you hear voices?"

"No." Time to give one word answers. Didn't want to run my mouth and end up saying something that could land me a room at the funny farm.

"Do you have visions?"

"After my dad died I saw him once. Clear as day. It was really neat." So much for one word answers.

"That's pretty common after a death, when you're grieving. When did your father die?"

"Four years ago, of lung cancer. It was pretty horrible."

"Yes, that's a horrible disease. Ali, I'd like to put you on an anti-depressant. I'm sure you've heard of Prozac?"

"Sure. One of my sisters takes it, sixty milligrams a day."

"I'm not going to start you off with that much. I'm..."

"Heavens no. She's totally neurotic. Oops, sorry, didn't mean to interrupt."

"That's okay. Go ahead."

"That was all. Just that my sister and I are really different." Rambling again. I began to worry that I may be wearing a little white jacket soon if I didn't keep my mouth shut.

"I'm going to start you with twenty milligrams, then I'll see you back in about four weeks and we'll see how that's working. I'm also going to give you Trazadone to help you sleep."

"Okay." I straightened up in the chair and looked right at him. I didn't want him to think I wasn't taking this seriously. I felt like I was in school again. Yes sir, no sir.

"Ali?"

Something in his voice made me nervous.

"Yes?"

"Eric tells me you've been smoking Marijuana and taking pills."

"Um, yes. Just a little is all."

"How much is just a little?"

"Only a joint here and there. Not even every day. Just occasionally. The pot helps me relax."

"What about the pills? What are you taking and how often?"

I squirmed in my chair. "Hmm. Well, nothing serious. Just Darvocet, Percodan, Xanax; those kinds of things. I'm not doing any club drugs. And I take them less often than I smoke pot."

"How long have you been smoking Marijuana?"

"I started when I was about sixteen, so I've been smoking off and on for thirteen years I guess. Then this past couple of months I started smoking more regularly. I'm not really sure why."

"I see. You realize for Eric and me to be able to help you, you have to stop. Today. Will you do that?"

"That makes me a bit nervous. I need some way to calm down, to relax."

"That's why I'm giving you these prescriptions. It'll take about ten days before you notice any difference. Will you promise me that you won't smoke any more Marijuana or take any more pills?"

"That really scares me. How about you give me ten days?"

"You know I can't do that." He paused, "But I'm not going to follow you home either."

"Okay." I felt like a schoolgirl being chastised by my teacher. For some reason, though, I wanted to please him. He radiated kindness.

As he made notes in my file I sat looking around his office. Framed documents covered part of the wall to my left and a full bookcase covered the opposite wall. I noticed one book titled "Memory, Trauma, and Treatment." Bet that was interesting. Another was titled "Psychology and Law." Yuck. How boring.

He handed me two prescriptions. "Remember, you won't be able to notice a difference for at least a week. Even then, it will be very subtle. Take one Trazadone shortly before you go to bed to help you sleep. If you're still awake in one hour, take another one. You can take as many as three."

"Okay," I said, trying once again to show how mature and serious I was.

"Good. I'll see you in about four weeks then." He stood and opened the door.

"Thank you," I said. But for what, I wasn't sure. For not kicking me out of his office? For not yelling at me? For not calling the cops? How far did this confidentiality thing go?

Chapter 6

It was only 2:00 when I arrived home from Dr. McCain's office. I had that anxious, unsettled feeling again. And, again, I felt like my life was being controlled by someone else. I stopped at the mailbox to retrieve the bills, walked into the house, tossed the mail onto the table, and headed straight for my stash. I lit a joint and took a Xanax. Better make the most of the next ten days. I smoked while I went over my session with Dr. McCain. Ten days, huh? I could do that. Anyway, if the medicine helped I wouldn't need the pot to relax. And I had no doubt that anytime I wanted to stop taking pills I could do it effortlessly.

I got a nice buzz, put a Sinead O'Connor CD on the stereo, and lay on the floor with the headphones on. I had plenty of time to come down before Alex would be home. Didn't want him to be pissed off. He hadn't been pleased with my recent behavior.

I closed my eyes. The phone rang. Damn. I paused the CD and picked up the phone. Thank heavens for Caller ID. It was the office. Couldn't be talking to them while I was stoned. Besides, I didn't relish the interruption of my high. I let it ring through to the voice mail. Taking advantage of the music being paused, I went into the kitchen to make myself a drink. I spent the afternoon smoking and drinking until I fell asleep on the floor. I woke up just before it was time for Alex to arrive home. I quickly emptied the ashtray and put it away, then hurried into the bathroom to have a look in the mirror. My eyes were bloodshot and I had a serious case of bed-head. I brushed my teeth, squirted Visine in my eyes, ran a brush through my hair, and put on some lipstick. It wasn't exactly a *Cover Girl* photo op, but it would work.

I heard Alex's key in the lock just as I walked back into the living room.

"Hi Darling." I gave him a kiss. "How are you?"

"I'm fine." He gave me the once over. "How are you?" Uh-oh. I knew that tone. He wasn't happy. Stupid of me. What had I been thinking? The house probably reeked of pot. I should have lit a candle or something.

It wasn't that I was actually trying to hide my use. Alex knew I was smoking more often, I just didn't want to flaunt it. He was quite upset about the recent turn of events. He thought I was reliving my crazy years, which he had tolerated once before. He wasn't too thrilled about a second round. We had an unspoken agreement that I wouldn't smoke in front of him.

"Did you have a good day?" I asked, trying to sound nonchalant.

"Yes, it wasn't bad."

"You hungry?"

"No, not right now. Think I'd like a cocktail first."

"I'll fix us both one. How would you feel about pizza tonight?

"Sounds good."

"Pizza and rent a movie?"

"Sure." He didn't seem to be as upset with me as when he first walked in. Maybe he wouldn't say anything.

Alex headed toward the bedroom to change clothes while I headed to the kitchen to mix our drinks.

We took our usual positions in the living room with him sitting in the leather chair, me on the couch, Van Morrison on the stereo.

"So how was your day?" I asked.

"Nothing exciting. I have to go to Phoenix sometime next month."

"You don't know when?"

"No. I think in a couple of weeks."

"For how long?"

"Two nights."

My first reaction was that I'd miss him. I hated it when he was gone. But a separate part of my brain leaped in another direction, telling me I could get high more often if he wasn't home. How sick was that?

"Which presentation is it?" I asked, feeling ashamed.

We continued to visit while we drank a second cocktail, then went to the video store to rent a movie.

When the pizza arrived we sat in front of the television eating and watching *Bowfinger*. After stuffing myself with three pieces, I tried to talk myself out of eating another, but failed. The pot had made me hungry. What a pig. No wonder I was overweight. I even pretended

I wasn't going to eat the fourth piece. I took one bite and set it back down. Then a few minutes later I took another bite, and so on, until the whole slice was gone. I considered wrapping the leftovers in foil and putting them in the refrigerator for emergency midnight munchies, but finally succeeded in shoving them down the garbage disposal.

After Alex went to bed I tried the same controlling method with the pot. I'd been so rattled when I left Dr. McCain's office that I'd forgotten to get my prescriptions filled. Technically, I figured, my ten days hadn't started yet. They'd start first thing in the morning after I picked up my medicine. Until then I'd just smoke a little to relax and maybe take another Xanax before going to bed.

Three hours later I went to bed totally stoned and somewhat tipsy. Oh well. Couldn't be perfect. Tomorrow I was going to start a whole new program – no pot or pills at all, eating right, walking five days a week, or maybe four. I really had to put an end to this stupid behavior.

I stumbled to bed and snuggled up close to Alex. I needed to feel the coolness of his skin against mine. He stirred and draped his arm over me. "You smell like Marijuana," he said and turned away from me.

Chapter 7

I woke up feeling fantastic Monday morning. When I checked my e-mail there was a message from the office saying they had a new project for me. That was good news. My crazy phase had kicked in over the week-end and I couldn't stay busy enough.

Four weeks later I was still on my mental high. I was only sleeping about four hours a night, getting up early in the mornings, working the whole day, then experimenting with new recipes for supper. When I wasn't working, cooking, or hanging out in bookstores, I was watching movies with Alex while I knitted. I wasn't smoking any pot or taking any pills. I was having three or four drinks at night, but not every night. I was happy. Alex was glad to see the old me was back. Because I was feeling so great I rescheduled my appointment with Eric. I tried to remember why I'd started going to therapy in the first place.

I'd seen Dr. McCain again and had been able to tell him that I'd kept my promise. I'd stopped smoking and taking pills after the ten days had passed. I didn't mention that I was drinking occasionally. I figured that information was on a "need to know" basis, and I didn't think he needed to know. I told him I couldn't tell any real difference with the Prozac, but he said I should continue with it for awhile.

My next appointment with Eric rolled around. It seemed odd to be seeing him when I was feeling so great. What were we going to talk about?

When I walked into the waiting room a woman was sitting in my violet chair. I stood there a second, not quite sure where to sit. I wanted to ask her to move; explain to her that it was my chair. How bizarre. Now I was claiming other people's furniture as my own. Guess I'm a bit more crazy than I realized. I finally took a seat on the couch and put my headphones on. I'd come to realize that I wasn't going to be able to read while waiting for my appointments so I'd brought music instead. I sat with my head back, eyes closed, listening to the new *Bush* album. I'd been there about fifteen minutes when Eric called me into his office.

"Hello Ali. How you doing today?"

"Hi, great. I feel fantastic." I took a seat on the couch this time. Eric sat diagonally across. Maybe he was going to suggest that I didn't need therapy after all. That I was cured.

"That's good. What brought this on? You think the Prozac's helping?"

"I really don't think so. I think I've just finally gotten back into my crazy phase. It's nice. I'm getting a lot done, but not sleeping much."

"Is the Trazadone not helping?"

"That's probably part of the problem. I'm not taking it till about 1:00 in the morning."

"Why are you waiting till so late?"

"It's just that I have to force myself to take it because I don't want to go to bed." I picked up a child's puzzle that was lying on the couch and began to turn the pieces so all the colors lined up. "I stay up till I can hardly stand it any longer, then I finally force myself to go to bed and take a Trazadone."

"Why do you think you have such an aversion to going to bed?"

"I don't know. It's weird. It's just that the minute the sun sets, I wake up. I can be tired and dragging all day, then boom, I'm wide awake."

"Do you have any idea why that is?"

"I just don't like night time. I can sleep in the day without any problem. It's just that I get crazy at night. I don't normally sleep during the day, but I can if I want to."

"When you do go to bed what happens?"

"I lie there for ages, tossing and turning, feeling anxious and apprehensive. Even after I take a Trazadone. Last night I ended up taking three before I finally fell asleep. That was after three hours."

"Why don't you make a point to take the medicine every night at the same time? Say, about 10:00, no matter what. I think it's important for you to set up a pattern."

"I mean to, but then I don't do it. I'll try again."

"And you can't think of any reason why you have this reluctance to go to bed?"

"No. Well, maybe." I stood up and began pacing. "I don't know."

44

"Did you have your own bedroom when you were growing up?"

"Why?"

"Just wondering." He hesitated a moment. "Did you?"

"I shared with my brother until I was nine, then we moved and I got a room of my own." I stood next to Eric's desk, staring out the window. It was a beautiful cloud floating day.

"Why did you move?"

"That's when my mom married my step-father."

"Did you always have your own room after that?"

"Yes."

"What else has been going on with you?"

"I really don't know what to say. I've been working a lot, staying busy. I feel great. I feel like I'm wasting your time being here."

"Have you been writing?"

"Yes, some."

"What are you working on?"

I sat back down and started playing with the child's puzzle again. I played with it awhile, then tossed it back on the couch, only to pick it up again a few seconds later.

"About when I was a kid. Summers at my grandparents' farm. Stuff like that."

"And that brings back pleasant memories?"

"Yeah, it was great then. We spent every summer there. I like writing about it. It puts me in a good mood. And the more I write, the more I remember. I love it."

We sat and talked and, as always, I worried. Had I gone past my allotted 50 minutes? Was he trying to stay awake? Was he wishing I'd just shut the hell up? Was he preparing his case notes in his head? *Rambles on and on and on.* When I finally shut up we discussed the date for my next appointment. I convinced him I could go three weeks on my own.

I walked to my car slowly, thinking about our session. When I'd arrived at his office I'd felt on top of the world. When I left I felt an undercurrent of anxiety. I couldn't explain it or understand it. Maybe I wasn't cured yet.

Chapter 8

That night I got stoned. The first hit I took was fantastic. Why had I quit these past few weeks? Why was I letting Eric and Dr. McCain tell me I couldn't smoke or take pills? What was the big deal about getting high occasionally? Can't believe I bought into that whole "this is a bad thing" crap. So much for my ten day promise. Maybe Dr. McCain wouldn't question me about my use anymore since I'd told him I'd quit. Anyway, I mused, as I made myself a drink, it would be awhile till I saw him again. I'd stop before then.

The next morning I still felt anxious and unsettled and had a hangover to boot. It took some time before I felt well enough to log on to the mainframe to work. At noon I'd surpassed my day's goal so I took the rest of the day off.

I logged on to the Internet to check e-mail. There was one from Pam and one from Leslie, but I didn't feel like spending time to answer them now. I ate a sandwich. I called Matt, but he wasn't home. I stood in front of the bookshelves and stared at the books. I lit a joint. Just to have a couple of hits to calm me down.

I was careful not to smoke too much. I wanted to be in complete control when Alex arrived home that evening. I made sure the house was straightened, candles lit, ashtray put away, and myself presentable before he walked in the door. Everything went well. I don't think he even suspected.

We had a pleasant dinner, then sat and talked while we finished a second bottle of wine. After we cleaned the kitchen I took a shower. When I returned to the living room Alex had spread a blanket on the floor, lit a fire in the fireplace, and made us each a cocktail. We spent a pleasant romantic evening and didn't get to bed until 1:30 a.m.

The next morning I awoke groggy and with a hangover, feeling depressed. I ate breakfast, worked about two hours, made the bed, hurried through the few bills that needed paying, then emptied the dishwasher. No matter what I did, I couldn't get past the feelings of anxiety and despair. I couldn't believe I felt so bad after the wonderful evening Alex and I'd had. I was so anxious at one point,

I thought I was going to throw up. Finally, I just gave up and lay on the floor listening to music and crying while I smoked a joint and had a few drinks.

When Alex walked in from work he found me lying on the living room floor, totally stoned. I didn't care. I spent the evening in my office smoking and playing computer games. I'd definitely fallen into my crash and burn phase. What had happened? How had I lost that "on top of the world" feeling so quickly? And how could I get it back?

I sat up till 3:00 a.m. waiting for the radar in my brain to alert me that it was safe to go to bed, that I'd be able to sleep.

I stayed stoned, half-drunk, and depressed the better part of the next two weeks. Alex was decidedly unhappy, but concerned, as well. I kept reassuring him that I'd be alright. Just not at that moment; that it'd have to be a little into the future.

My next appointment with Eric wasn't for another ten days, but I decided I'd better not wait that long if possible. I dialed his office number at 2:00 a.m.

"You've reached the voice mail of Eric Bradshaw. If this is an emergency, press zero for immediate assistance. To leave a message press one. Thank you."

I pressed one.

"Hi Eric. This is Ali Connery. I was just wondering if you had any time available this week. I feel like I need to see you. I'm not doing too well. But if you don't that's fine. I understand. It's not an emergency or anything, but I'd appreciate it if you'd give me a call. The number's 237-0039. Thanks. Sorry to bother you."

I finished my joint, gulped the last of my drink, and went to bed.

Eric called the next afternoon. He had an opening the following day.

I sat in the waiting room with my headphones on. When Eric tapped me on the shoulder it startled me. I hadn't heard the door open. I was embarrassed, too, to be caught off guard.

"Hi Ali. Pretty good music?"

I jumped up from the chair as I jerked the headphones off. "Uh-huh," I mumbled.

He walked ahead of me, opening the door into his office. "So

48

what were you listening to? Looked like you were enjoying it."

I took a seat on the couch. "Oh, Alanis Morrisette, *Bush, Matchbox 20*. Alex refers to it as 'that crap Ali listens to.' He thinks I'm going through my second childhood."

"What do you like about that type of music?"

"I don't know. It's passionate, raw."

"Do you always listen to rock?"

"No. Mostly when I'm in my crash and burn phase."

"Like you are now?"

"Yes."

"When you're listening it seems as if you're almost in a trance. Do you feel that way?"

"Yes, I love it. I'm completely drawn into it."

"What do you do while you're listening at home?"

"Lie on the floor with my headphones on. Don't check e-mail. Don't answer the phone. Don't call anyone. Don't go out. Just listen."

"Is that what you've been doing?"

"Yes."

"For how long?"

"About a week." I stared at the throw pillow in my lap. "Well, maybe ten days."

"Ali?"

"Yes?" I looked up at him.

"Have you been smoking pot and taking pills again?"

Damn. Was there a sign on my back? I tossed the pillow aside. I sat back on the couch with my arms folded in front of me, legs crossed. "Yes, a little." I waited for the lecture.

"What do you think precipitated your mood change?"

Wow. I couldn't believe it. He let it slide. Maybe he really did understand. "I'm not sure. It seems like it started after our last session. I don't really know why, though. Don't even remember what we talked about last time."

"We talked about your reluctance to go to bed."

"Oh, yeah. I don't know then. Don't know why that would set me off." I picked up the pillow again.

"What kind of routine did you have growing up?"

49

"What do you mean?"

"After school. Going to bed. Those kinds of routines."

"Oh. Well, first thing when we got home from school Mama always had a snack for us. Chocolate chip cookies and milk or something. After changing clothes we'd have our snack, then do our homework. After homework, we helped with supper, either cooking or cleaning. Then we watched television or went outside to play until bedtime. I'm not sure, but I think bedtime was about 8:30 or 9:00."

"Did your mother and step-father tuck you in? Or did they just tell you goodnight and you went to bed?"

"Mama always tucked us in. Jack, my step-father, would usually just tell us goodnight in the living room, give us a hug and a kiss, but sometimes he came in later to say goodnight."

When I left Eric's office I forced myself to go by the grocery store to figure out something to fix for supper. I hadn't been cooking since I'd been in my crash and burn phase. We'd been living on salads and cereal.

I was in the kitchen when Alex arrived home around 7:00.

"Hi. Smells good." He walked over and gave me a kiss. "What is it?"

"Hi. Pork tenderloin. How're you?"

"Great. I had a good day. How about you?"

"I'm okay. I saw Eric today."

"Oh, that's right. How'd that go?"

"Interesting. I'll tell you while we eat."

We sat and talked during supper. I told him about my meeting with Eric and tried to explain the feelings of unease and depression I couldn't seem to get rid of.

"I'm sorry you're feeling so bad, sweetheart. But you've been smoking a lot lately, haven't you?" he asked.

Why'd it always have to come back to that? "Not too much," I answered.

He leaned forward in the chair. "What do you mean not too much? You're getting high every day, aren't you?"

"Well, yeah."

"But you don't think that's too much?"

"No, not really."

"How much would be too much, Ali?" He stared directly at me. I stared back. I could play that game, too. "I don't know. Besides, I'm going to quit soon, so it won't matter."

"Oh? When's that going to be?"

"I don't know yet. But soon."

"How about today?"

"Well, I already got high today so it can't count. Maybe tomorrow."

"Yeah, sure." He stood up, grabbed the plates from the table, and stormed into the kitchen. Damn good thing he didn't know about the pills.

I stayed at the table, defiantly, and finished my glass of wine.

We watched television for a couple of hours while I labeled and put pictures into a photo album. Alex barely spoke to me. I didn't care. As soon as he went to bed I made myself a drink, went into my office, and lit a joint.

Eric had suggested I keep a journal. "Nothing elaborate," he said. "Only enough to put down your feelings; what's going on with you." He thought I might be able to spot a trend or see a common thread in my moods.

I sat at my computer trying to think of what to write. That I was high as a kite? That I loved it? That I felt like screaming when I wasn't stoned? I was so high I kept forgetting what I was going to write. When I remembered and finally got something down, I kept having to go back and fix my typos. I typed for ages it seemed.

After writing in my journal, I took my position on the living room floor with the headphones on, listening to music, replaying my conversation with Eric. The more I thought about it, the more I began to recall childhood memories. Silly stuff with my brother and sisters. Playing Monopoly on the living room floor. Racing on our bicycles. Playing football in the front yard. Making up skits.

Then I had flashes of Mama. Ironing. Baking. Sweeping. Oddly, I had few varied memories of my dad or Jack, my step-father. Mostly I remembered Daddy coming home from his trips with gifts. Daddy being drunk. Daddy's unwarranted jealous rages. Daddy pulling a gun on Mama. Jack grounding us for misbehaving. Jack taking me shopping. Jack buying me panties. Jack having me model my new panties. Weird hazy snatches of scenes from long ago.

For the next two weeks I tried everything I could think of to bring myself out of my black mood. I went to bookstores. I wrote. I took pictures. I walked. I worked. Nothing helped. I couldn't shake it. I waited anxiously every night for Alex to go to bed so I could get stoned, then wrote in my journal while I listened to music.

I slowly began to feel better and regained my mental high at last. I didn't quit smoking completely, but cut down on my use. I was busy looking for books, cooking, working, and cleaning. We started going out with friends again. And again I tried to remember why I had ever started going to therapy.

Alex was excited to see I was feeling better, but was upset and concerned that I was still getting high. I kept telling him not to worry, that I'd change soon, get back to my old self.

When I arrived at Dr. McCain's office it took all my will power to take a seat in the waiting area. I felt more like jumping up and running down the hallway.

"How're you doing today, Ali?"

I knew now that it was just polite chatter till we got into his office and I answered appropriately.

I took a seat on the couch this time. I realized he always waited for me to sit down before he sat. I wonder where he'd sit if I went for the recliner. Would he move his chair? Probably just turn it toward the recliner. For the first time I noticed that his furniture was arranged so all he ever had to do was swivel and he'd always maintain the same distance and position. Guess that's something they teach you in shrink school. How To Arrange Your Furniture 101. I wasn't bold enough to sit in the recliner. That seemed too relaxed. Like I should be searching for the remote control and flipping through the television guide.

"So how've you been feeling?"

"Right now I feel fantastic. Can't do enough at once. Feel like I need to run around the block. I'm in my crazy phase."

"Have you been feeling like this since I last saw you?"

"Actually, no. Only about the past week or so."

"And before then?"

"I was in my crash and burn. Pretty bad, too. I haven't really sunk that low in quite awhile."

"Did something happen to precipitate the mood change?"

"Which one? The up or down?"

"Either of them. Was there some trigger that you can remember?"

"Not really. I was feeling great, went to see Eric, then fell. Hard. Now I feel great again."

"I'm going to change your Prozac to thirty milligrams a day. I'd like to see if this new dosage will help even out your mood swings. I have some information here, too, about being Bipolar. Although your mood swings aren't as severe and you're not truly Bipolar, I think it will give you a better understanding of what you're feeling, and about the recurring depression."

"Okay."

"How's your sleeping? Is the Trazadone helping?"

"Yes."

"I want you to continue to take the Trazadone at night then, and the Prozac in the mornings."

"Okay."

"Have you had any thoughts of suicide?"

"No."

"Thoughts of hurting anyone?"

"No." It always freaked me out a little when he asked those questions. I understood it was part of his job, to make sure I wasn't so far on the edge I was starting to lean in the wrong direction, but it still unnerved me just a bit.

"Is your husband being supportive?"

"Yes, thank goodness. Don't know why he puts up with me."

Dr. McCain gave me a smile and continued. "How are your sessions with Eric progressing?"

"Good. We're talking some about what it was like when I was growing up."

"Is there anything else you want to discuss today?"

"No. I'm pretty much okay right now."

"Okay then. I'd like to see you back in about six weeks. To see how this dosage is working."

"Okay." I stood up and took the new prescription from him as well as the Bipolar information pamphlet. I stuffed them both in my purse. I'd made it through the session without him asking about my drug use and was anxious to get out the door before he pulled a Columbo.

He opened the door for me. "Take care, Ali."

"Thanks," I answered. Again, unsure why. For increasing my Prozac? For giving me prescriptions? For keeping me on drugs till I regained my sanity?

Chapter 9

I had the luxury of another two weeks in my crazy phase. I'd caught up on all the petty chores that needed doing, had finished the baby blanket I was knitting, and had gone out to dinner a couple of times with girlfriends. I needed something more to occupy my time. I hung out at the local hardware store, dreaming about how I'd redecorate the guest bathroom. I walked up and down the aisles selecting flooring, cabinets, faucets, and tile, envisioning how the finished room would look if I really had the money to buy everything. I eventually bought a bucket of paint.

At my previous appointment with Eric we had spent the session talking about my childhood memories. He said talking about them and writing about them would cause more memories to come to the forefront of my conscious. He was certainly right. I began to have strange recollections during the oddest moments; while I was in the shower, driving down the freeway, cooking supper. I felt like an amnesiac glimpsing scenes from a play. I knew the play was about me, but I felt detached at the same time. I fell into a deep depression and couldn't figure out why. What had happened this time?

I began smoking pot on a daily basis again, staying stoned the better part of each day. I was also taking whatever pills my dealer had available. When I started losing my zone I panicked and hurried to light another joint or take another pill. Alex was upset, but I didn't care. When I didn't have work to do, I spent the days lying on the floor, drinking, while I listened to music.

I wrote furiously in my journal. In my crazy phase I only had time for quick, brief notes. In my depression I wrote long rambling philosophic bullshit laced with anger. I was beginning to feel like a Jekyll and Hyde character. Or like I had some evil twin. What the hell was wrong with me?

Once again I left a 2:00 a.m. voice mail for Eric. "I need you."

When I awoke the next morning I resolved to stop smoking pot altogether. After all, it was a depressant and I didn't need any outside stimulus to hasten my downward spiral. I forced myself to sit down and pay some bills, wash a couple of loads of laundry and give the kitchen a good scrubbing. I felt like I was going to jump out of my skin.

That afternoon I went to a head shop and bought a pipe. So much for my resolution to quit. It hadn't lasted six hours. I tried out the pipe as soon as I arrived home. Alex came home to find me stoned and lying on the living room floor crying.

The next day I worked for a couple of hours before I tried some other diversions. This time I cleaned both bathrooms, wrote in my journal, and went grocery shopping. I couldn't stand it any longer. My skin was crawling with anticipation. I popped a couple of Xanax and smoked while I put the groceries away.

Half an hour later I remembered to check messages. Eric had called. He had a cancellation and could see me that night at 7:00. If I was able to come I didn't need to call, he'd just wait for me. I looked at the clock. Damn, not very good timing. I was enjoying a nice buzz; 7:00, huh? I did a quick calculation and decided I'd be okay to drive by 6:30 if I didn't smoke anymore.

I sat in my violet chair in the waiting room, afraid I might've made a mistake in coming while I was still high. I considered leaving before Eric saw me, quickly jumping up, running out the door, down the corridor, and to my car.

Eric opened the door. "I see you got my message."

"Yes, hi. Thanks for calling." I walked into his office.

"What's going on with you? You sounded a bit frantic on the phone."

I slouched on his couch, my feet stretched out in front of me, my hands locked behind my head. I was enjoying the remnants of my high. I told him about the depression, how I felt like I was going to jump out of my skin, and about the memories that kept popping into my brain.

He leaned forward in his chair, his hands clasped. "Ali, are you high right now?"

Uh-oh. Didn't think it was noticeable. "Ummm. Just a little."

"You drove here?"

"Yeah. I was okay. I waited till I thought it was safe. I almost turned back, but I felt like I really needed to see you."

"How do you plan on getting home?"

"I'll be alright in a little while."

"We'll see. What's so urgent?"

I stood up, then sat back down again. "I know why I'm afraid sometimes."

"Oh?"

"Something happened when I was twelve years old."

"Did you just remember this?"

"No. I was just too embarrassed to mention it before."

"Do you want to tell me about it?"

I stood up again and stared at a picture on his wall, my arms crossed in front of my chest, my back to him. I didn't answer.

"Ali?"

"Yeah, well, you see, when I was twelve my cousin and one of his friends made me, uh... Well, actually, it was my cousin's idea. He told me... He said I had to give him and his friend a blow job. When I asked what that meant they both cracked up laughing, telling me how stupid I was."

"Where did this happen Ali?"

"In some old house we were exploring. It was abandoned and we'd heard an old lady had died there. We thought it might be haunted or something, you know. We were there, exploring, like I said, and we were upstairs on the second floor and I was so scared I just wanted to leave, but I was afraid to go downstairs by myself. Scared some ghost or someone would get me. That's when they told me."

"Told you what they wanted?"

"Yes. That if I didn't do it they'd leave me there. In the house. That they'd lock me in the closet and leave. They made me get on my knees." I swiped at the tears in my eyes, too embarrassed to turn around to reach for a tissue. Neither Eric nor I spoke. I just stood there crying.

"Was it at night?" He finally asked.

"No, the middle of the afternoon. Afterwards I threw up. I cried all the way home. My cousin told me I'd better shut up or he'd make me do other stuff. That's when my nightmares began."

"Did it happen more than once?"

"Oh yeah, for ages. I don't remember exactly. I don't understand why I kept going places with them. Why didn't I just stay away? I thought they liked me. And I wanted to feel important, hanging out with older kids. But I don't understand why I kept going."

"Was that your first sexual experience?"

"No, not exactly."

"Can you tell me about your first experience?"

"Oh, God. I don't know."

"How old were you?"

"Eleven."

"What happened?"

"My cousin started screwing me."

"The same cousin?"

"Yeah, Scott."

"How old was he?"

"Seventeen."

"How long did that go on?"

"I'm not sure. A few years, I think. I was so ignorant I was afraid I was going to get pregnant and he had to explain to me that it wasn't possible. He thought that was pretty funny. That I was ignorant, I mean. You see, I hadn't... well, you know. I was just a kid. When I had to give them each... When I did the other thing for the first time, I did his friend first and his, um... Well, he wasn't ready. I'd never seen one that wasn't ready before and I thought something was wrong with it. Like it was broken or something. They thought that was hilarious. Told me to put my mouth on it and it would grow. I was disgusted. Thought I was being clever by putting my finger in my mouth then touching my finger to him, but he knew it wasn't the real thing and said I had to put my whole mouth around it."

I sat back down on the couch, tears streaming down my face. My hand was shaking when I reached for a tissue.

"Have you ever told anyone this?"

"Only Alex."

"You never told your mother?"

"No."

"Why not?"

"I was too ashamed."

Chapter 10

I awoke the next morning with a migraine. When Alex woke up I asked him to get me an Imitrex.

"You want an ice pack, too?" he asked.

"Yes, thanks." I lay on the bed with a pillow over my head, crying.

Alex returned to the room. "You want me to fix you something to eat?"

"No, thanks. I think I just need to lie here awhile if you don't mind. Sorry."

"That's okay. I'm sorry you feel so bad. I assume you want the fan on and the lights out?"

"Yes, please."

I put the ice pack on my forehead and rolled over on my side. I couldn't stop crying. The pain became so intense I finally took a Valium to help me relax. I fell asleep. It was close to noon by the time I woke up.

"Hi there. How're you feeling?" Alex asked as I walked into the living room.

"Better, thanks. My headache's gone, but you know how it is. Now I feel groggy and worn out from the pain and medicine."

"Can I get you something?"

"No, thanks. I think I'll just lie on the couch."

"You must be starved. You want something to eat? I'll go get you a malt if you like."

"No. I don't think I could eat. I just want to lie here. Thanks, though. I appreciate you looking after me."

"Okay, then. Let me know if you change your mind. Will the television bother you?"

"No."

"Oh, how was your session with Eric yesterday?"

"Draining."

"You want to talk about it?"

"I don't think so. At least not right now."

I spent most of the day on the couch. That afternoon when Alex went to shoot pool I popped a Percodan in my mouth, washed it down with vodka and 7, then lit my pipe. The Marijuana enveloped me and I lay on the couch savoring it until I fell asleep. I woke up when I heard Alex's key in the door. Good thing I'd had the presence of mind to put my stash and accessories away earlier.

I fell into a deep depression and had to force myself to function on a day-to-day basis. I got high and drunk every evening as soon as Alex went to bed. I forced myself to act responsibly during the day, working, paying bills, grocery shopping, cleaning house. Alex and I went out with friends, went to the movies, went to dinner, but I was detached and looked forward all day to when Alex would go to bed. As soon as I heard him sleeping, I fixed a drink, then pulled out my stash.

The night before my next session with Eric, I sat in my office reading the pamphlet Dr. McCain had given me about Bipolar Disorder. Once again I read the symptoms; fatigue, loss of energy, diminished interest in activities, feelings of worthlessness during the depressive phase, followed by decreased need for sleep, racing thoughts, increase in goal-directed activity, blah, blah, blah in the manic phase. Don't know why I kept reading the damn thing. Hell, I could've written it. I was living it. Although I wasn't bipolar, my mood swings were extreme and I think I just needed to know someone out there understood what I was going through and to be reminded that there was a flip side to whatever phase I found myself in at the time.

I dreaded seeing Eric the next day. I was embarrassed about some of the things I'd said to him earlier and couldn't remember other things. I wasn't sure what to expect as I sat waiting for him.

"Ali, come on in."

"Hi. First I want to apologize for my behavior a couple of weeks ago." I said. "It was wrong of me to come when I was stoned. I'm sorry."

"Okay."

I began to pace his office floor.

"How've you been feeling?" he asked.

"Not too great," I answered, and immediately began rambling about my depression, how I couldn't shake it. How my crash and burn phase wouldn't go away. How I felt like I was wallowing in a black hole. How I was spewing vitriol when I wrote in my journal and didn't understand where it was coming from. That I seemed to have all this anger in me, but didn't tap into it unless I was stoned or drunk. Then it was virulent. Told him 2:00 a.m. seemed to be a particularly bad time for me, and was he sure he couldn't see me then? He laughed and said it just so happened that 2:00 was when he was doing his best sleeping.

We discussed my love of music again and he suggested I try changing the music I listened to when I was depressed. Suggested I listen to the music I would normally listen to when I'm feeling good. See if I could pull myself out of the depression. He also gave me some guided imagery techniques to use to try and calm myself.

Finally the depression slipped away. I felt fantastic and cut down considerably on my use of pot, pills, and alcohol. My appointment with Dr. McCain came sooner than I wanted, though. I'd intended to quit getting high completely before our next session, but hadn't been successful. Otherwise I would've looked forward to the meeting. Dr. McCain seemed like he genuinely cared about me and my well being. I'd wanted to have a good report for him if he asked. Maybe he wouldn't.

We didn't get far passed the usual hi, how are you, before I began rambling about the black hole I'd been in and how I was back on top of the world now. I was in talk mode and nothing short of patience and good timing could stop me. When I paused for breath, he jumped in.

"When's the last time you smoked pot, Ali?" Just like that. Out of nowhere; didn't even fit into the context of what we'd been talking about.

My stomach flipped. I hesitated. Should I tell the truth? That hesitation was all it took. He stopped writing and looked straight at me.

"Ali?"

"A few days ago."

"I thought you'd quit. Wasn't that our agreement?"

"Yes."

"How long is a few days?"

"Uh, about five, or maybe three. No, four. Yeah, four sounds right."

"How long have you been smoking again?"

"Awhile. But not every day," I reminded him.

"Are you still drinking and taking pills?"

"Yeah, but not very often," I lied.

"You realize that's a deadly combination?"

"I know, but I'm careful and I don't do it all the time."

"It only takes one mistake, Ali. I can't continue to give you medicine if you continue to use drugs, especially when you're adding alcohol to the mix. You understand that, don't you?"

"Yes."

"Do I need to send you to rehab?"

"Oh, God, no! It's not that bad."

"I'm going to increase your Prozac and I want to give you a small dose of another medicine to take at night instead of the Trazadone. Although I don't want you to completely lose your highs and lows, I'd like to stabilize them so they're not so extreme. I can't do that, though, unless you promise me you'll quit smoking Marijuana. You also have to quit the pills and alcohol. Will you do that?"

"Yes," I answered timidly. He'd scared the hell out of me with that rehab talk. It wasn't like I was a drug addict or an alcoholic.

"The medicine will help, Ali, if you let it." He handed me the new prescriptions and we both stood up. I was crying. "We're going to help you through this," he said.

"I know. Thanks."

I made a determined effort to completely quit all the pills, pot and alcohol. It went well for about a month. My sessions with Eric were becoming more intense. We'd discussed my sexual experiences a couple more times, but not in any great detail. I knew, and I think Eric knew, there was more to discuss, but I couldn't bring myself to talk about it.

Looking back now, I'm not exactly sure what happened. All I know is that I woke up one day and realized I couldn't stand the anxiety any longer. I felt like I was dancing on a tightrope. After Alex left for work that morning I got stoned. And, oh my God, it was glorious.

Chapter 11

The office didn't have any new projects for me so I was working very few hours. Once again I spent my days stoned and my evenings stoned and drunk, with a few pills thrown in for good measure. On the morning of my next appointment with Eric, I got high and fell asleep on the couch. When I awoke I dressed for my session, grabbed a plastic container from the cupboard, made myself the equivalent of four drinks, and rushed out the door. I sipped on my vodka and 7-Up as I drove, then sat in the parking lot and guzzled down what was left. By the time Eric called me in I was well on my way to drunk. I started talking as soon as I was in his office.

"Did I ever tell you about Jack, my step-father?" I asked. "How he used to tuck me in?"

"No, you mentioned he would occasionally come in later to tell you goodnight. After your mother did."

"Yeah, well, he had a special way of tucking me in." I hadn't even bothered to sit down. I stood staring out the window again, my back to him. "When I was already asleep he'd come creeping into my room, then wake me up so he could tell me goodnight. Like when you're in the hospital and they wake you up to give you a sleeping pill. He'd stroke my hair. It was long, down to my waist. He told me how pretty I was and what a good kid I was, always behaving, always minding. All that crap. Then he'd tell me to take off my pajama top so he could see if I'd started developing yet. Those were the words he used. Then he'd run his hand across my chest. Of course, I mean, it was stupid. I was only nine years old. There wasn't anything to feel or see."

"I thought your first sexual experience was with Scott."

"Yeah, you're right, I did say that. How odd. I don't guess I ever figured what Jack did to me in the beginning was a real sexual experience. I mean, he was my step-father and I was just minding him."

I stood there, my back to him, not wanting to move, not even to wipe away the tears that were rolling down my cheeks. "I've decided I must emit some sort of sound that only assholes and dogs can hear that says 'here I am, use me.'" I turned away from the window. "Fuck him. Fuck everybody. I hate men."

"You hate all men?"

"Yes," I answered vehemently. "Well, of course not. Not all men. Most of them, though. They're mostly all assholes. Not you, of course. Or Alex, or some of our friends. But most all the others. They disgust me."

"I assume you never told anyone about this either?"

"Nope. No one. Well, except Alex. And I haven't told him everything."

"Are you still in contact with Jack?"

"Hell, no. My brother and sisters are, though." I began to feel sick at my stomach. "I need to get out of here. I need to get high."

"I don't believe you're in any shape to drive."

I didn't think he'd noticed my state of near inebriation. Maybe I wasn't as clever as I liked to think.

"How long did it go on, Ali?"

"I dunno. Ten years maybe. I mean, hell, he was still doing stuff to me when I was an adult. How sick is that? Why did I continue to see him? Even after he and Mama divorced I'd go visit him. That's really twisted."

"What did you do when you went to see him?"

"He usually took me out to lunch or dinner."

"Then what?"

"We'd go back to his apartment."

"What would happen then?"

"I can't talk about that now." I sat down. "Oh, God, I just realized."

"What's that?"

"Sometimes when I got home I'd find money in my purse! Oh my God. I always thought he was just being nice, feeling sorry for me 'cause I was always so broke. What an idiot. He was fucking paying me. I really do need to get out of here."

"Why don't you tell me about some of the men in your life who have treated you well? Who are they?"

"There's Alex, of course. My family thinks he saved my life."

"Why is that?"

"When I met him I was doing a lot of drugs. You know the drill. Downers to help me relax, then speed to wake me up. Acid and Ecstasy for the hell of it. By the time I was fifteen I'd figured out if I gave guys what they wanted, they'd give me what I wanted. Drugs and alcohol. When Alex came along I was pretty fucked up. He refused to play my little game. I did weird stuff, like drop acid before he picked me up for a date. We wouldn't be able to go anywhere then except his apartment 'cause I was tripping. He'd just sit there with me till I came down, then take me back home. And he'd have to go to work the next day. I used to pick fights with him, too. Tried everything in my bag of tricks to show him what a horrible person I was. He finally told me one day that he wasn't going to leave no matter how hard I tried to push him away. That I was worthy of being loved. Sweet, huh?"

"Sounds like he came along just in time."

"Yeah. He wouldn't put up with my destructive behavior and it finally came down to either him or the drugs and alcohol. Don't know where I'd be otherwise. Our friend Matt's the same. Known him as long as I've known Alex and he's always treated me well. He's seen me in all my craziness, too. And there's Daniel and a couple others."

"So there are a few nice guys out there."

"Yeah, I know. A few. I get so angry, though, 'cause men have to turn everything into something sexual. I'm sick of billboards and television commercials and radio ads where it's always some guy trying to get laid. Sometimes just the thought of sex turns my stomach."

"Even now? With Alex?"

"Well... Oh, God. I really don't want to talk about this."

"Why don't you just finish what you started to say."

"Well... Oh, crap. Now... Well, I can't seem to get interested in making love unless I'm stoned or drunk." I flung the words out. "And that really scares me."

"Why is that?"

"'Cause that's the way I used to be. When I met Alex. I viewed sex as a tool. He was really patient with me, though. Kind of helped me reprogram my thinking. But now I'm feeling like I did when we were dating."

"Does Alex know how you feel?"

"No. At least I haven't mentioned it. He may've guessed." I started crying and sat holding my head in my hands. "I really need to get out of here and get high. I just need a joint so I can feel better." I sat there for several minutes, crying, neither of us speaking. I stood up. "I have to go."

Chapter 12

I stopped at the liquor store on my way home from Eric's office. I got home at 5:30, made myself a strong drink and rolled a joint. I smoked while I looked through my collection of pills, trying to figure out which one suited my mood. I was looking forward to sitting back, relaxing, and becoming totally wasted, putting my thoughts on hold.

Once again I was stoned when Alex arrived home. He wasn't pleased at all. He barely spoke to me. The next few days I tried to stay away from the drugs, but I just couldn't do it. I fell back into my pattern of smoking, drinking, and taking pills every night after Alex went to bed. I continued to write in my journal, passages of drugged induced ramblings about men being assholes, about me wanting to be high during my crash and burn phase, and about how great I felt and how wonderful life was during my crazy phase. Surely, only a total lunatic could write such rubbish only weeks apart from one another.

The next appointment I had with Eric was very subdued. While spouting my drunken mouth off in the previous session, I'd said more than I intended. No telling what the hell he'd written in his case notes after I left.

It was time to see Dr. McCain again and I was really dreading it. Why couldn't I pull myself together? I prayed we would have a quick meeting to check my medicine and that he wouldn't ask any questions about the drugs and alcohol.

I was cheerful and carefree when I greeted him, smiling so wide I thought my lips would crack. Didn't want to give any clues as to my real state of mind.

"So how're you feeling, Ali?"

"Good, great."

"The new medicine working?"

"Yeah, it seems so. I'm sleeping well. Everything's great! I still have highs and lows, but they're not nearly as extreme. I'm good."

"Have you quit the drugs and alcohol as you promised?"

Crap. I couldn't believe it. "Well, no, not really. My sessions with Eric have been pretty weird. I need to be able to calm down."

"Life's going to throw you curve balls, Ali. That's not an excuse."

"I mean to do better, then I just don't." I looked at him, beseechingly, I hoped.

"How often are you using?"

Using. What a ridiculous word to apply to what I did. Addicts *used*. I simply partook of a few chemical pleasures.

"Ali?"

I didn't say a word.

"Every day, huh?"

"Yes."

"Both pot and pills?"

"Well, I don't take pills every day. Depends on what I can get my hands on. It's really not a big deal."

"What about drinking? You doing that every day, too?"

"Yes," I finally answered, my fake smile completely faded.

"That's it. I'm sending you to rehab."

"What? No!" I started crying. "Please don't do that."

"Sorry, but you leave me no choice."

"Please give me one more chance. I swear I'll quit. I'll really do it this time."

"I've given you enough chances already. It's time for me to be the doctor and take control."

"But I'll really quit this time. I promise."

He didn't bother to answer, simply looked down at his legal pad and began writing. "I want you to go over there right now. I'll call them and tell them to expect you."

"Dr. McCain, please. I don't want to."

He looked up at me. "Ali, if you don't do this I'll have to stop seeing you. I can't continue to treat you while you're using drugs. I've told you that before."

"But it's not a big deal, I swear. I just do it for fun. I can quit if I really want to." I stared at him, tears streaming down my cheeks.

"Too late."

"Damn, damn, damn." I sat on his couch, bent over, rocking, with my arms wrapped around my waist.

"It's only for a few hours a day. I'll see you over there every week. And I want to see you here in my office in three weeks. I want to keep you on a short leash for awhile."

I swiped at the tears streaking my face. I was embarrassed to walk back out into the waiting area.

I sat in my car in shock. Rehab? What the hell had I done? Alex was going to freak out. What should I do? I could just not go. But then what? I felt like Dr. McCain and Eric were helping me. I was getting things out of my head for the first time and my mood swings weren't as severe as before and they occurred less often. I just didn't want to stop getting high. Why'd everyone have to make such a big deal about a little pot and a few pills?

I followed the directions Dr. McCain had given me to Whispering Pines Hospital. What a name. Sounded like something out of a "B" movie from the 50's. I was surprised I found it so easily. I hadn't realized his words had sunk in past my panic. I found a place to park and somehow got my legs to move in the appropriate manner to allow me to walk.

I took a deep breath and opened the door. There were couches and chairs; a few people sitting or standing around the waiting area. Were they all drug addicts? Or were they visiting poor desperate souls who'd been put away for awhile?

"Hi. I'm Ali Connery," I said to the receptionist sitting at the desk. "Dr. McCain sent me over for an evaluation." I tried to sound calm, self-assured.

"Hello. Sign the book please and fill out this form. Someone will be with you shortly."

I took the clipboard and sat down in a chair away from everyone else. I filled out what I now recognized as the standardized North American Doctors' Form and handed it back to the receptionist. I took a seat again. Ten minutes later a woman, about 45, tall, with wispy blonde hair, greeted me.

"Mrs. Connery?"

"Yes, hi."

"Hi. I'm Melinda Rivers. Will you come with me please?"

We walked to a set of locked double doors. She used a card pass to unlock them and I followed her through. For a split second the thought passed through my mind that I had one last chance to bolt and run. I was too timid, though. *A+ in "Follows instructions well."*

She showed me to a small room with a table and three chairs. "I'm the admissions director, Ali. I just need to ask you a few questions and take care of some other formalities, then a nurse will be in to talk to you."

What exactly did she mean by take care of some other formalities? Wasn't that what they always said in those 50's movies right before someone was declared insane and committed? Maybe this was all a hoax and I'd walked onto a movie set. Everyone was playing their roles very well.

Melinda took my blood pressure, temperature, and pulse while she asked me questions. "Why has Dr. McCain sent you here today, Ali?"

I considered not answering, telling her to figure it out for herself, but decided it wasn't the time to be obstinate. "He thinks I smoke too much pot and take too many pills." I didn't mention the drinking.

She pulled out a flashlight and shone it in each of my eyes. "Are you high right now?"

"No." Of course not, I added to myself.

"When's the last time you got high?"

"Last night."

"Okay. Just sit back and relax. Rebecca will be here soon. Would you like the door closed?"

"No, thanks." Although I wasn't crying, I was still a bit shaky.

"Can I get you some water or anything?"

"No, thank you."

I sat there impatiently waiting for half an hour, becoming angrier by the minute. Twice someone popped in to say that Rebecca would be right with me. Maybe this was part of my audition. Another half hour passed before I met Rebecca. She was also tall with wispy blonde hair. Wonder if that was the notice for the casting call. All nurses must be tall with wispy blonde hair, but will take any manner of whacked-out lunatics to play the role of patients.

After we made it past the contrived pleasantries, she got down to business. "First thing I need to do is take your picture. If you'll just stand up against that wall." She picked up a Polaroid camera.

Holy shit. These people were serious. I didn't even pretend to smile. I just stared straight into the camera, wondering what the hell I was doing there. She took two pictures. What was she going to do with them? Pass them around the hospital? Here, take a look at the newest nut. Hang them in the post office? Throw darts at them during break? Maybe they had a good behavior "nut of the week." My picture would be displayed in the lobby and I'd get to park by the front door for a month.

"Dr. McCain called to let us know you were coming, but he didn't say where you were supposed to go. Do you know?"

"I'm not sure. He just said for me to come for an evaluation and that I'd be here a couple hours each day." I wasn't about to mention that he'd said something about chemical dependency. I didn't figure my part in this little movie called for me to volunteer any information. If she was so great, let her figure it out herself.

"Okay, so he doesn't want you admitted to the hospital."

Oh, Lord, no, I wanted to shout. "No, just day stuff," I answered.

She took out all kinds of legal documents for me to read and sign. Insurance forms and that sort of thing. There was a lot of red tape involved in becoming a loony. After all the paperwork was completed, she sat back in her rolling chair and I sat back in mine across the table from her. If anyone would've seen us in another setting they probably would have assumed we were two colleagues having a friendly chat after lunch, except Rebecca was drilling me about my history and discovering my drug use and how often I was getting high. Guess she was better than I thought.

For myself, I still wasn't buying in to the idea that Marijuana was a real drug or that I took enough pills to be called an addict. I told her I got high every night and, yes, I drank some, and, yes, I took pills occasionally. After our little chitchat I followed her back through the locked doors, passed the receptionist, to another set of locked doors, which she unlocked effortlessly with her magic card.

"I'm going to take you over to Unit Two. A unit supervisor will show you around."

I walked behind her, still feeling like I was in some sort of surreal, phantasmagoric, you're on Candid Camera type of setting.

People were milling about on the lawn smoking cigarettes or

standing in groups talking; some sat on benches reading while others spoke on cell phones. Didn't look too bad. Reminded me of a school campus.

We entered the doors marked "Unit 2" and Rebecca introduced me to Chloe, who also fit the casting call perfectly. I'd come across a *Stepford Wives* institution I decided, and it was all becoming a bit too spooky for my taste.

Chloe took over for Rebecca and showed me around; a water fountain, the ladies room, a room for my purse, a Coke machine. About a dozen people straight out of central casting were sitting or lying on couches or chairs. One person was writing in a notebook, another was reading a novel, and still another was lying on a couch with headphones on. Chloe told me to have a seat, that she'd be right back, they'd be starting "group" in a minute. I took the nearest seat, rather like a game of Musical Chairs, hoping not to be caught out.

Within five minutes Chloe returned and took a seat. The others put away their diversions and came to life.

"Everyone, this is Ali." She nodded in my direction. Some of them nodded, some said hello, and I nodded and answered in return. I felt like an idiot; first day in school, day one of a new job.

"John, you want to start today?"

And so it went. Me sitting there in a freaked out, shock induced daze, while people bitched because the other group facilitator wasn't there and because two groups had to be combined for that one session, and that it was too large and they didn't want to talk in front of people that weren't a regular part of their own group. Oh Lord, get me out of here!

Chapter 13

It turned out I only had to sit through that one group before the day was over and I was sent on my merry way with instructions to return the next day. After stopping at the grocery store for a few things, I spent the rest of the afternoon going over the day's events, trying to make some sense of the whole turn of events, and thinking about what I was going to say to Alex.

Was he going to be angry with me? Say I shouldn't have gone; should have just come straight home instead? Was I stupid to go just because Dr. McCain told me to?

Alex arrived home just as I finished putting the groceries away.

"Hi darling, how are you?" I gave him a kiss.

"Hi. I'm fine. Had a good day. How about you?"

I followed him into the bedroom. "Interesting, but I'll tell you about that later. Why don't you tell me about yours first?" I lay on the bed while he changed clothes and filled me in on everything happening at the office.

All through supper I avoided talking about my day. I wasn't sure where to begin and was nervous about Alex's reaction.

"Shall we finish this off?" Alex asked, holding up the bottle of Merlot.

"Sure, why not."

"So, you haven't told me about your day yet. You saw Dr. McCain today, right?"

"Yes."

"Well, how'd it go?"

"It was interesting."

"Yeah, you said that. What made it so interesting?"

Figured I might as well just spit it out. "He sent me to rehab."

I studied Alex's face and didn't notice even the slightest change of expression. Damn. He was good. Must be the training. Psychology 201 – never, under any circumstances, show shock or horror or surprise or disgust. Learn to disguise all emotions.

"That *is* interesting. What were the events that led to that decision?"

73

I told him how Dr. McCain was concerned that I was getting high every day. How he'd warned me before that he couldn't continue to medicate me if I was going to continue to use drugs and how freaked out I was about the whole thing. "Are you mad?" I finally asked.

"Me? No. I think it took a great deal of courage for you to go through with it."

"Really? Thanks."

"I've been really worried about you, sweetheart. I haven't said much, hoping you'd just work it all out, but I've been very upset. I don't know what's going on with you anymore."

"I know. I'm sorry. I'm just going through some weird stuff, with the therapy and all, I mean."

"Yes, I know. But that's no reason to get stoned every day." Once again I was grateful he didn't have any idea about the pills or that I'd been drinking daily. For the hundredth time I wished pot didn't have such a distinctive aroma and I could smoke to my heart's content.

"I know that," I mumbled. "I just keep thinking I'll wake up one day and stop. At least that's been my plan. I don't know, I feel like this is just a temporary setback I'm going through."

Alex poured more wine for us each. "I'm glad you're going, sweetheart. I really do think you need some help. You kept telling Dr. McCain you'd quit and didn't so it's obvious you can't do it on your own."

"But I really think I can eventually. And I still don't see what the big deal is." I was almost pleading. "Why is everybody so upset?"

"Are you being serious?"

"Yes."

"Let's see. Oh yeah, because it's illegal!"

"Besides that, I mean."

"What do you mean, besides that? It *is* illegal."

"Okay, I know. But let's pretend it's not. Then what's the big deal?"

"First of all, it is. You can't simply pretend it's not. But it affects you, Ali. You sit up till all hours of the night getting stoned and playing computer games. That's not like you. You're depressed. You're not participating in life. You're staying away from all your friends. You're not taking pictures anymore. Hell, you're not even reading or going to bookstores. And in the evenings you can hardly wait till I go to bed so you can get stoned. Don't think I haven't noticed."

"I know. But it's just the therapy."

"No it's not, Ali. Stop using that as an excuse. I'm sure the therapy is unsettling and you're talking about some difficult issues, but that doesn't give you license to smoke Marijuana every day."

"I guess not."

"So you go back to rehab tomorrow?"

"Yeah. Isn't that just too exciting?"

"I love you, sweetheart. I know you can do this."

"Thanks. I love you, too. Sorry I'm putting you through all this right now. But if you'll just be patient with me, I know I'll make it through."

We finished the bottle of wine. I stood up and gave him a kiss on my way in to clean the kitchen.

He began clearing the table. "So what kind of hours do you go?"

"It's from 9:00 to 3:00 every day. I started late today, of course, so I only went to one group. But we're supposed to have a "this is how I'm feeling today" kind of thing at 9:00 with everyone present. Then we break into two groups, about six to eight people in a group. We eat lunch and have more groups. Something like that. I'll know more tomorrow, of course."

We both cleaned the kitchen as we continued our conversation.

"You want to play some cribbage?" Alex asked over the roar of the dishwasher.

"No, I don't think so. Do you mind if I just go in my office? I want to write in my journal. I feel a bit weird. I guess I need to iron something to wear tomorrow, too."

"No, of course not. I thought you might like the distraction."

"Thanks, but I don't think so. I don't think I could concentrate on anything else right now. Alex?"

"Yes?"

"You're sure you're not mad at me?"

He slipped his arms around me. "Of course not, sweetheart. I'm proud of you. What you're doing isn't easy. I love you," he said.

"I love you, too."

Chapter 14

I arrived at rehab the next day nervous and anxious. I couldn't believe I was going to have to spend most of the day there. The receptionist told me to sign the book, write in Unit Two as my destination, and to write down the time of my arrival. She gave me a red badge that clipped to my clothes, identifying me as a patient. Wonderful. I actually got to advertise the fact that I was there as one of the whackos instead of as an employee or a visitor.

She buzzed me through the locked doors, allowing me access into the inner whacko sanctum. I walked into the large open room where the day's activities would start. By the time the opening scene began, there were about fourteen of us and the group facilitator. Each of us had to take our turn telling the others how we felt, which ranged from some people feeling great to others being severely depressed and almost non-communicative. Because I was busy rehearsing my part, I only heard snatches of other people's lines. Finally, I was cued.

"Uh, I'm just feeling a bit anxious," I said. "Not really knowing what to expect. Uh, other than that I guess I'm okay." Great. Don't think anyone would make the mistake of thinking I earned my living as an orator.

After a fifteen minute break from that little soiree, we broke into two separate groups. I was told to go with group "A." After someone told me which group that was, I fell in behind them and followed them to a small room in the back of the building. I was the last to enter and was able to watch the others vie for the couch or the comfortable chairs. The furniture formed somewhat of a circle, facing a whiteboard in the back of the room. Chloe came in and took a seat beside the whiteboard. She was our group's therapist.

Wesley began by talking about his depression and his wife's chronic illness and how he wished everything was like it used to be. Then Janice said she understood the other side of that coin because she'd been in a car accident and was dealing with constant pain and her husband didn't understand. I sat there listening, not participating, thinking I didn't belong there.

I was starving by the time we broke for lunch. The Instant Breakfast I drank that morning hadn't been enough to carry me through an anxious morning of group therapy. When no one asked me to join them at the group table in the cafeteria, I sat alone, reading, while I ate my cheese enchiladas. I didn't feel comfortable with them anyway.

After lunch we regrouped in the same back room for pharmacy instruction. That certainly sounded like something I'd have some interest in hearing. The hospital pharmacist came down to discuss and answer questions about the actions, reactions and interactions of Depakote, Prozac, Librium, Wellbutrin, Elavil, and an assortment of other mood altering drugs. It was quite an odd thing to be sitting there inside a hospital in the middle of a gorgeous Spring afternoon discussing drugs. It wouldn't have to get much more weird before I'd start having an out-of-body experience I decided. Unless I was having one already and just didn't recognize it for what it was.

At the end of the last session Chloe told me the unit director would visit with me the next day to set up a treatment plan. Great. Something else to look forward to.

While driving home that afternoon I carried on a conversation in my head with Dr. McCain, cursing him for turning on me.

I reluctantly returned the next day. Once again I ate lunch by myself. When the afternoon group ended, Chloe told me there had been some confusion as to where I was supposed to be because Dr. McCain had been called out of town on an emergency before they were able to discuss my treatment plan with him. Dr. Stevens, his associate, would be talking with me instead of the unit director. Uh-oh.

Dr. Stevens was about fifty, with thick, brown hair, not a gray strand in sight, and a Robert Redford mouth.

"Hi, Ali. I'm Josh Stevens.

"Hi."

"Let's see if we can find a room where we can talk."

I followed him past a couple of closed doors before we finally found a room that wasn't occupied. He entered first, taking a chair at the desk, while I sat in the only other chair, a couple of feet away. He turned his chair toward me, a file, presumably mine, in his hand

78

as well as a legal pad and pen.

"So, Ali. As you know Dr. McCain was called out of town, but he's asked me to chat with you."

"Yes."

"When's the last time you got high?"

Damn. He didn't waste any time. Got right down to it.

"Uh, two days ago, I guess. Yeah, night before last."

"I see. Have you been doing drugs for a long time?"

"No. I mean not now, nothing but pot and a few pills. Nothing serious. I don't really understand why I'm here."

"What about before? Did you take other drugs when you were younger?"

"Yes."

"Acid?"

Wow. He really didn't mess around. "Yes."

"Ecstasy?"

"Yes."

"Speed?"

"Yes." Were we going through the alphabet?

"What else?"

Once again I discussed the litany of drugs I used when I was wild and crazy. I made sure he understood that I didn't use any of those drugs now; that I only smoked a little pot and had an occasional pill or two, but no recreational drugs.

He was pleasant, but business like. He ended the fifteen minute session by telling me that the director of the CD, chemical dependency, unit would be over shortly to talk with me and for me just to wait there.

Looked like I was busted.

Carla arrived within five minutes. Didn't take these people long to get word out if they were really determined.

I spent another ten minutes giving Carla my history and listening to her discuss chemical dependency. She ended the session by pointing out where Unit Five was, the CD unit. I was to report there at 8:30 the next morning.

Damn. Here we go.

Chapter 15

While Alex watched television that night, I took a shower, made myself a strong drink, went into my office and closed the door behind me. I logged on to the Internet, took a couple of Darvocet, then lit my pipe. When Alex came in he glanced at my pipe, then back at me. He gave me a kiss and said goodnight before walking out. I'd seen the hurt in his eyes and I felt bad. But not bad enough to stop. I sat in my office smoking and drinking for hours. By the time I stumbled into the bedroom to go to bed I was already regretting the vodka I'd drank. I went to sleep about 3:30 a.m.. When the alarm clock rang at 7:00 a.m., I almost came off the bed. What the hell? I must be having a nightmare, must've entered the *Twilight Zone* while I was sleeping. Surely I couldn't be expected to actually get out of bed and get myself together to attend CD rehab. I pressed the snooze button.

I finally dragged myself out of bed at 7:30, the need for water winning over the need for sleep. Oh God. It all came back to me. It was real. I really had stayed up drinking and smoking and I really was supposed to report to rehab. Damn.

I took a quick shower to help me wake up and sober up, applied my make-up and fixed my hair. I slipped into jeans, a blouse, and tennis shoes. It was obvious I wasn't going to win any beauty contests, but I didn't think I'd cause dogs to start howling spontaneously either. I ran out the door with a Coke in my hand.

I arrived and signed the book at the receptionist's desk. Destination: Unit Five.

I walked into a totally different environment than I'd walked into at Unit Two. Men and women were lined up in front of a nurse sitting at what looked like a doctor's reception area. They were taking their medicines for the day. Past that was a large open community area with a dozen rooms opening onto it. One of the patients showed me around the common area. She explained there were currently eighteen people staying in the hospital in the CD unit, but there was room for twenty-four. There were two beds in each room. The patients generally stayed anywhere from two to four weeks, depending on their addiction and insurance.

"Have you been admitted already?"

"Oh, no," I answered, trying not to let the panic show through my voice. "I'm just supposed to come during the day."

"Oh, IOP."

"I'm sorry?"

"Intensive Out Patient."

"Oh."

She continued my quick tour, pointing out where to find the daily schedule of activities, the bathroom, and a Coke machine. After I completed the tour I took a seat on one of the couches and pulled a book out of my purse. A couple of people came up and introduced themselves and welcomed me, which I appreciated. When everyone was seated, a woman named Kathy began speaking. Seemed she was the day's group facilitator for the morning meeting. A different patient took on the duty every day. She started by explaining that today's meeting was going to begin with each person stating a concern for another person in the group, then stating an affirmation for someone in the group. You had to look at the individual when speaking and he or she wasn't to respond in any way. Weird.

Once again I'd been thrown into a situation where I had to say something before I even knew what the hell was happening, and once again I sat there rehearsing my spiel.

Almost every person in the group expressed concern for Billy, a cocaine addict, who was leaving that day for the outside world. He'd been in the hospital the past twenty-eight days. They reminded him how dangerous it was out there, to keep it simple, to make a lot of meetings, to stay in contact with the group, to stay close to his sponsor. I wanted to remind him not to cross the street without looking both ways, not to get into a car with strangers, and not to step on a crack or he'd break his mother's back. But I didn't of course. I was only a smart aleck in my head.

When it came my turn I said I was concerned for Kathy because she'd told me she was having some problems with her family. I then said that my affirmation was also for Kathy for taking the time to show me around, and to everyone else who had been kind enough to make me feel welcome. I don't think I made as big of fool of myself as I did my first day at Unit Two.

The meeting ended with us all standing together in a circle, holding hands, saying the Serenity Prayer aloud. Afterward several more people introduced themselves and asked me what my drug of choice was. "Marijuana and pills," I answered, feeling like a fraud since I didn't believe smoking pot and taking a few harmless pills was a serious enough offense to warrant rehabilitation. I wanted desperately to explain that I was only there so my psychiatrist would continue to see me.

After the morning meeting we broke into smaller groups. I was in Shirley's group. Six of us, seven counting Shirley, gathered together in a very small room that was furnished only with chairs. Almost everyone had a bottle of water either in their hand or sitting on the floor by their chair. Group rules were posted on one wall; the group must end at ten minutes before the hour, one foot must remain on the floor at all times, no leaning back in the chairs, no sleeping, no headphones, no books, no interrupting. No.... No... No...

There I was, just another day in paradise.

My group consisted of me, an alleged Marijuana addict and pill popper, a female speed freak, a male crack addict, a female heroin addict, and two alcoholics; one female, and one male. It was evident to me and anyone with a lick of sense that I didn't belong there.

Shirley started the group by welcoming me, then asked me to tell my story. When I finished my short speech she asked questions. How'd I end up in rehab? What was my drug of choice? What other drugs had I used? When was the last time I used? When I answered that I'd gotten high the night before, they all nodded. They understood the method behind the madness.

When everyone was satisfied they knew enough about me to allow me into their little club, Shirley asked if anyone had anything in particular they wanted to discuss.

Grace, the heroin addict, raised her hand. She was young, early twenties, very attractive, very thin, black hair, black eyes, and black nail polish. She sat in the chair with a white blanket wrapped around her.

"Yes, Grace?" Shirley asked.

"I'm still having a problem glamorizing my use. When I think

83

about it I keep remembering the fun I had and how great it felt." She looked around at the group.

"You can't remember the bad times?" Shirley asked.

"I remember 'em but put 'em out of my mind and focus on the times it was good."

"And the cost? How much were you spending?"

"Well, uh, I was doing a paper every other day."

"And how much does a paper cost?"

"About seventy-five dollars."

"And how did you earn the money to pay for your habit?" Shirley asked.

"Oh, different ways." Grace lowered her head. Tears fell as she pulled the white blanket tighter around her.

Shirley persisted. "You want to tell us about them?"

"I did some favors for people," she whispered.

"I'm sorry?" Shirley answered. "I'm not sure everyone in the group heard you."

"Favors," Grace repeated.

"You mean sexual favors?"

"Yeah. You know, the usual."

"Uh-huh, pretty glamorous life."

Grace didn't speak.

"I've noticed you always wear long sleeves." Shirley said.

"Yeah."

"Is that because of the tracks on your arms?"

Grace gave her a quick glance. "Well, yeah."

"If those were such great times, why are you hiding your arms? Why don't you roll up your sleeves and show everyone?"

You could've heard a pin drop. All heads turned toward Grace. She sat there, crying, fidgeting with the blanket.

"Grace? You want to show us your arms?"

She continued to stare at her lap. Slowly and hesitantly she rolled up the sleeves of her blouse. A couple of gasps were heard and one person actually put her hand to her mouth. Grace's arms were covered with big black and blue bruises at her wrists and elbows.

"Did you shoot between your toes?" Shirley asked.

"Yeah, pretty much anywhere I could find a vein."

"And this is the glamorous drug use you recall?"

Grace didn't answer.

After a few seconds another person in the group spoke. "I shot speed a few times and once when I was high I took pictures of my arms. Every time I wanted to shoot again I took the pictures out and looked at them."

"I've never taken any pictures," Grace answered.

"We have a camera at the desk," Shirley said. "Will you let me take pictures of your arms after group?"

"Okay." She rolled down her sleeves.

"When I got sober last time," the female alcoholic said, "I wrote down some of the worst things I'd done while drinking. I kept that list in my purse and read it when I wanted to drink. Maybe you could try something like that."

"That's a good idea," Shirley said. "I used to facilitate a group called Incident Therapy where each person had to write down three incidents that occurred during their use, then had to share them with the group. Would you be willing to bring an incident story to group tomorrow, Grace?"

"I guess so." She still hadn't raised her head to look at the group.

"You'll make the commitment to write it tonight and share it with us tomorrow?"

"Yes."

"Good. Does anyone else have something they'd like to discuss?"

And so it went with everyone sharing their fears and concerns and their desire to use, while the others tried to help them find a way to stay clean and sober one more day.

Get me the hell out of here!

Chapter 16

I must admit I immediately felt more comfortable with this group of people than the ones I'd been with the previous two days. I felt a sense of kinship with them.

When it was time for lunch they were all very solicitous, making sure I knew where the cafeteria was and asking me to join them at the table reserved for Unit Five. We had a pleasant lunch, talking about kids, careers, and everyday life, pretending we weren't all sitting in a fricking rehab with a bunch of other addicts.

After lunch, both groups convened in one large room for CD Instruction. We watched a film about addiction, then a therapist, who was also an addict, presented more information on addiction and answered questions. He assured us we weren't there because we were bad people, but because we each had an allergy to alcohol or some other drug. Our bodies didn't handle chemicals the same way a "normal" person's did.

"I'd like you to raise your hand," he said, "if you have at least one parent that's an alcoholic or addict."

I raised my hand.

"Now, don't anyone put your hand down. I want you all to look around the room and see how many hands are raised."

I turned my head. Every single person in the group, probably 25 people, had a hand raised.

"See," the speaker said. "That's not a normal distribution. You would never have that kind of skew in a room full of everyday people. You can put your hands down now."

"Statistics show that if you have one parent who's a substance abuser, you have a 25% chance of becoming an abuser yourself. Two parents equals a 50% chance, which is as high as it goes. So you see, you're not bad people. You haven't misbehaved. You have a disease."

Incredibly enough I actually enjoyed the lecture. It was quite informative. But I still didn't see myself as an addict and I made mental adjustments when the lecturer spoke about those other poor souls in the room.

I took advantage of the break after the lecture to sit outside and read my book. I'd given up on *Sacajewa*, not having the patience for it at that time, and had started *Bridget Jones's Diary*. I was enjoying it immensely, reluctant to put it down to attend another group session with a bunch of drunks and addicts.

In the afternoon session, Shirley had to occasionally wake up Bobby, the speed freak. He'd been awake for two days and had just checked into the hospital that morning. He was exhausted and the medicine they gave him made it worse. I felt sorry for the poor guy.

The male alcoholic started the session by saying that his wife had attended the family meeting last night and caused quite a stir. Evidently she'd disagreed with some point the chairperson made and was quite vehement in defending her position. As the drunk and the crack addict told the story together, careful not to interrupt each other, I sat back and watched. One of them actually stood up to demonstrate one of the finer points of the night's activities. I felt like I was watching a high school play. Like I was an audience member in a roomful of amateur actors. Surely it couldn't be real. It was all just too, too weird. What the hell was I doing there?

I didn't participate much the whole day. I spoke when asked a direct question, but for the most part kept my mouth shut. I certainly didn't want to slip up and say something incriminating while sitting in group therapy in the middle of a rehab hospital. Mum was definitely the word.

We ended the group in much the same manner as the morning meeting and the previous group, only this time we recited The Lord's Prayer instead of the Serenity Prayer.

After group, everyone met once again in the common area. This time we each had to say what kind of day we'd had, how we were feeling. The day patients had to say what they planned on doing when they got home. Did they have some activity to tend to? Were they having thoughts of using? (Duh! We were in rehab!) Did they have someone to call if they had the sudden urge to drink or use drugs? Were they attending a meeting that night; Alcoholic's Anonymous, Narcotics Anonymous or Marijuana Anonymous? I had a strong desire to tell them I was attending a meeting, but that it was Anonymous Anonymous so I wasn't at liberty to discuss it any further. In the end I had to confess I wasn't attending any meeting at all. Hell, I just got into CD that day. I was still trying to learn the damn jargon.

"Ali, do you still have some Marijuana and pills at home?" Shirley asked.

"Yes," I answered reluctantly.

"I'd like you to go home tonight and throw it all away. Will you do that?"

My whole body went cold and I think my heart may have actually skipped a beat.

"I don't know. I, uh..."

"It's important, Ali, that you don't have any temptations. Please tell me you'll get rid of it all."

All eyes were on me. Talk about peer pressure.

"Okay," I finally answered.

"And your pipe."

"Do I have to?"

"Yes. That's the only way to do it. All at once."

"You want someone to go with you?" another person in the group asked. "I'll do it for you if you like."

Oh my gosh. These people were fucking crazy! Like I was really going to let some stranger into my house to throw away my drugs. I could just picture him walking in with gloved hands held upright, like a surgeon, mask in place. "Take me to the contraband. I shall destroy it."

"Ali?"

"Okay. I'll do it."

"You promise?"

"Yes."

"Good.

We ended the meeting with the Serenity Prayer, which I desperately needed at that point. With that little task behind me, I was ready to bolt for the nearest exit. As I gathered my purse and book, trying not to be too obvious in my haste to depart, Shirley approached me.

"Ali. How'd the rest of your day go?"

"Okay, I guess."

"I'm really concerned about you. Do you think you could make a meeting tonight?"

I stood there dumbfounded.

She picked up a blue booklet laying on the table next to us. "Here's a schedule. What part of town do you live in?"

Oh my gosh. She was serious. "Uh, Southeast. But I won't be able to make a meeting tonight."

"Why not? There's a Marijuana Anonymous meeting on that side of town at 7:00."

"Well, I've already made plans for the evening. We're going out to dinner with friends."

"Yes, I heard you say that. But you have to get your priorities in order. Staying clean is the most important thing right now."

God, how I hated the jargon. *Clean*? How stupid. Would they get off it already? It was just some damned pot and pills! What was the big fucking deal? You would've thought I was smoking crack every few minutes while I smuggled cocaine over the border so I could hang out at schoolyards trying to entice young children into joining me in the underbelly of society.

I was amazed at my successful effort to control my shock and annoyance. "I understand," I finally answered. But I really can't go tonight." I moved closer toward the exit. "I'll see you tomorrow," I said. Please just get me out of here.

"Ali, wait. Have you done your UDS?"

"I beg your pardon?"

"Urine Drug Screen. We do random tests."

"Oh, no. But..."

"I know. You got high last night. But we still need to do it. We need a baseline."

I can't say for sure, but I think my mouth may have dropped open.

"Let me get you set up." She motioned for me to follow her behind the desk where a young man was busy filing charts. "Andy, this is Ali Connery. She needs a UDS."

I nodded.

"Hi Ali. There's someone in the bathroom now, but when he comes out, you're next. Just take this cup in there with you." He pointed to the bathroom door on his left. "When you're finished, give it to me."

I took the plastic cup and waited, staring into space. When the man came out of the bathroom, I just stood there like I was slow in the head and needed someone to explain to me the procedure I should follow to cause my body to move in a forward direction.

"Ali?"

"Yes?"

"You can go in now. The bathroom's available."

"Oh, thanks."

I sat on the toilet, plastic see-through cup in hand, trying to figure out what I ever did in my life that caused me to end up sitting in a strange bathroom in a rehab hospital, a man practically standing guard outside, waiting for me to hand him a cup of my urine so it could be checked for evidence of drug use. The world had definitely turned upside down.

I finally completed the task at hand, walked out and gave my precious fluid to Andy. I desperately wanted to tell him to handle it with care, that it was of great value, but I didn't. Instead I headed straight for the exit. Do not pass go. I was buzzed through the locked double doors to the outside world where I signed out. I'd made it through another day.

Chapter 17

I wasn't scheduled to meet with Eric for another week, but knew there was no way I could wait that long if I was going to go through with this rehab bullshit. This time I didn't wait until 2:00 a.m. to leave him a message. I called as soon as I walked in the door. Expecting to get his voice mail, I was surprised when he actually came on the line.

"Eric, hi. It's Ali Connery."

"Hi Ali. How are you?"

"Well, have you talked to Dr. McCain?"

"No, why?"

"He sent me to Whispering Pines!"

"Uh, oh. You locked up?"

"No. IOP."

"How's it going?"

"Horrible. I hate it."

"Well, you know what you need to do."

"I know, it's just not that easy right now. I was calling to see if you had any time available this week."

"Hold on just a second, I'll check." I heard him open his desk drawer. "I've got something Friday morning at 10:00. Will that work?"

"Yes, great. I'll see you then. Thanks."

I felt calmer after hanging up and immediately went to my hidden cache of pot. I considered flushing the pot down the toilet, but couldn't bring myself to do something that drastic. Instead, I grabbed all the pills, the pot and my pipe with one quick and merciless movement and threw them into the trash. There, I thought. No big deal.

That night after Alex went to bed I sat in my office trying to stay busy. I longed for a joint or maybe a Xanax to help me relax. I couldn't believe I'd been so stupid as to throw everything away. What kind of dumbass thinking was that?

I played computer games while I considered digging through the trash. I hadn't taken anything out of its plastic bag. It wouldn't be that difficult to find it all. But only someone with a real addiction would do something like that. I made myself a nice strong vodka and 7-Up instead. I certainly didn't have a problem with alcohol. I could take it or leave it.

I decided I should ask Eric if I could see him every week while I was going through rehab. I needed someone to talk to and Alex wasn't the answer. Not right now. Not my husband.

I told my supervisor at rehab that I had an appointment Friday and wouldn't be able to make it in. She wasn't pleased, but there really wasn't much she could do about it.

"So, what's going on with you?" Eric asked the second we were in his office.

"Dr. McCain sent me to rehab. I can't believe it!"

"What happened?"

"When I saw him last time he asked how often I was getting high."

"And?"

I started pacing the floor. "Well, when he guessed that it was every day I said yes. It's my own stupid fault for telling the truth. I just can't believe he really sent me. I begged him for another chance. Told him I'd really quit this time. But he said he'd given me plenty of chances already." I sat back down on the couch. "I just can't believe it."

"I'd say you had fair warning."

"Oh, I know."

"What else is going on?"

"Nothing really. I'm still having dreams that someone's trying to hurt me. I'm still afraid of the dark. I'm still spending my energy fighting flashbacks. I'm not cured, yet. I thought I'd be well by now."

He chuckled at that bit of idiocy. "What else can you tell me about Jack?"

"Oh, God. I hate talking about him." I covered my face with my hands.

"I know it's not easy, but keeping it inside is worse. You need to talk about it to lessen the power it has over you."

94

"I don't know what to say. Can't you just ask me yes or no questions? Then I can just sit here and answer."

"That doesn't usually work very well. I don't know what to ask and don't know what you're ready to discuss. You've told me that he started coming into your bedroom when you were nine."

"Yeah." I picked up the pillow.

"When did things progress past him touching your chest?"

"Oh, God. Not for awhile. Looking back now it seems he built up very slowly. I mean, when he first started touching me I didn't realize it was wrong. I think that's one reason I didn't say anything in the beginning. I just didn't know. Then it progressed slowly, so by the time he was actually having sex with me it seemed almost a natural thing, and by then I was ashamed I'd let it continue so long."

"Can you tell me what happened next?"

I tossed the pillow back on the couch and stood up to take my position in front of the window, my back to Eric.

"He always told me what he was doing was for my own good. That he was teaching me about my body. Ha. One night when he came in it was different. I was ten or eleven, I'm not sure. Anyway, he did the usual stuff, stroking my hair, touching my chest, but that night he told me to pull down my pajama bottoms." Heat suffused my body and my stomach did a little flip. I turned my head and glanced at Eric. He was sitting in his chair, leaning forward a bit, hands clasped, looking at me with genuine concern and compassion in his eyes. He didn't say anything.

"God I hate talking about this." I turned back toward the window. "He told me to pull down my pajama bottoms and he touched me. At first he only rested his hand there, you know. That went on for awhile, weeks I think, maybe months, I don't know. Then eventually he started... Oh, crap. He, uh... It's really hard for me to say this. It's embarrassing."

"Don't worry about that. I can guarantee it's nothing I haven't heard before. Just spit it out."

I let out a sigh of resignation. "He put his finger inside me. After getting me used to that, he started doing more. Using two, then three fingers. Told me he was helping me; preparing me for when I was married and started having sex. It wouldn't hurt then, he said,

95

because of him helping me now."

I paused. Eric still hadn't spoken.

"You know, the stupid thing is I believed him. I think that's why I didn't consider it a sexual experience; more of a biology lesson. I really thought that was normal. Of course, who was I going to ask? My girlfriends? 'Hey, does your dad or step-dad come into your room at night and stick his fingers up you?' Right. Fucking asshole." I walked over to the table and grabbed a tissue. "Why did he do that to me? I just don't understand. I keep going over and over it in my mind, this neverending video. But I can't figure out what I did wrong."

Eric spoke very softly. "Ali, it's important for you to realize it wasn't your fault. It wasn't anything you did. You didn't cause it."

"I know that – intellectually. I keep telling myself that. But it still feels like it's my fault." I dabbed at my eyes with the tissue.

"Why?"

"'Cause I didn't stop it."

"But that's what abusers do. They manipulate you. Tell you it's for your own good. You eventually come to believe that you asked for it and that it's your fault if you don't like it."

"Part of me hates him so much I can hardly stand it. Another part keeps saying it wasn't that bad. And the Christian person in me wants to forgive him. But I can't right now. I hate him too much. Both of them. Jack and Scott."

"I don't think you're ever going to be able to forgive him or Scott, Ali, until you talk about it. Get it out and stop blaming yourself. Put the blame on them, where it belongs."

"I know, I know." I paced back in forth. "But sometimes I feel this murderous rage from the depths of my soul that I can't seem to control and that scares me. Then sometimes I just lie awake in bed replaying the scenes over and over in my mind like some sick broken film. You know, it's kind of funny, in a twisted sort of way, that my cousin was already screwing me by the time Jack worked his way up to that part of my lesson. I'm sure he'd be pissed off if he knew Scott beat him to it." I sat down on the couch and looked up at Eric. "Am I ever going to get over all this?"

"It doesn't ever go away, Ali. You just learn how to live with it."

"Oh, God, I hate this."
He reached for his appointment book. My time was up.

Chapter 18

I continued my daily journey to rehab and continued hating it. After I'd been there about a week, Shirley approached me and told me that my insurance didn't want to pay for IOP. That I was being transferred once again. This time to Relapse Prevention Therapy. It was from 10:30 a.m. to 2:30 p.m., Monday through Thursday. Yahoo!

She took me to another room and introduced me to Joe Mendoza. He looked to be about thirty-five years old, maybe five feet, nine inches tall, chunky build, straight black hair and a long nose. Not what one would call handsome, but not homely either. Just average. He seemed pleasant enough, but I knew better than to let my guard down.

Before long, others started filing in and taking a seat in Joe's office. There were seven of us, including Joe. Joe sat at his desk, his chair turned toward the rest of us sitting in a semi-circle in metal fold-up chairs. Looked like the less time the therapy lasted, the less comfortable the furniture was. He glanced up at the clock.

"I'll give Juan two more minutes." We all sat there in silence.

I looked around his office. It was pretty shabby in terms of furniture and not very neat. Papers were strewn on his desk. A metal, library-type bookshelf held books at all angles. There were posters placed strategically on the walls; First Things First, One Day at a Time, Keep It Simple, Let Go and Let God, and other AA slogans. I felt like I was in some kind of warped variation of an army recruiting office. "AA Wants You."

"Okay, that's it, folks. Jimmy, you want to close the door please? Doesn't look like Juan's going to join us today. Everyone, this is Ali." He gestured toward me and the rest of the group nodded. "Ali, you want to tell us a bit about your history and what your drug of choice is?"

Here we go again. Same song, fourth verse. I told my story. I was through in record time. I'd become very efficient in giving my drug induced autobiography.

Joe leaned back in his chair. "So, how's everyone doing today?

99

Huh? How about you, Jimmy?"

"Hi everyone. I'm Jimmy, a crack addict."

"Hi Jimmy," everyone responded in unison, except me.

He was really adorable, in that way some men have of always looking like a little boy, naïve and innocent. In his late twenties probably and cute as a button. Maybe I could fix him up with my niece. Oh, jeez. There I was in rehab trying to figure out a way to fix my niece up with an addict. Good. Real good. Just what she needs. And how would I explain where I met him? Oh, yeah, didn't I tell you I spend my days on the west side of town with drunks and addicts? Sorry. Guess I forgot to mention that.

"I'm feeling great today," Jimmy said. "Went to a meeting last night with my sponsor. The NA meeting over on 34th. It was good. Going to see my sponsor tonight to work on the fifth step."

"That's good. Real good. How 'bout you, Simone? You make a meeting last night?"

"Hi. I'm Simone, and I'm an alcoholic."

"Hi Simone." Once again I didn't join in the requisite response.

"Yes, I went to an AA meeting. Got my thirty day chip!"

"That's great! Good for you!" Everyone praised her.

"Yeah, I'm trying to do ninety in ninety."

Jake turned to me and said "ninety meetings in ninety days." I smiled my appreciation in being filled in on this bit of jargon.

Joe went around the room to each person, asking how they were, did they make a meeting, what were they feeling. All that bullshit.

The man next to me nudged me and handed me a clipboard holding a piece of paper, a sign-in sheet.

Column one--Name? That was easy enough. *Ali*.

Column Two--Thoughts of Using? How fucking stupid. Of course. Why the hell else would I be there? *Yes*, I answered.

Column Three--Attend a meeting yesterday? *No*.

Column Four--Have a sponsor? *No*.

Column Five--Contact your sponsor yesterday? *No*.

Column Six--Additional Comments? *I'm here*.

I handed the clipboard to the woman next to me.

"We're going to discuss triggers today," Joe said. "It's important for all of you to realize what events can trigger a backslide; the everyday things in life that addicts react to by using. Jake, can you tell me a trigger?"

"Sure. Fighting with your girlfriend or wife, or whatever."

"That's right," Joe answered. "It's easy to use that as an excuse. You have a big fight, you storm out and think, 'I'll show you, I'll just get drunk' or 'I'll just get high.' Right, Ali?"

"Huh?" I almost came off my chair. I'd been listening, but only with one ear. I was actually thinking about how I could score some other drugs. The pot and the prescription drugs weren't really doing the trick anymore and I was ready to move up to something else.

"Oh, yeah, sure," I finally had the sense to answer.

"Can you name another trigger?"

"Oh. Well, a bad day at work, I guess." Don't know where that came from. I worked at home.

"Good. That's right."

"Simone, how 'bout you?"

"Getting too tired?"

"That's excellent. Yes, that one's a bit subtle. It's important that you don't let yourselves..."

I tuned him out. How much more boring could it get? Wonder what it's like to do heroin. I don't think Grace's going to make it. In fact, I'd give five to one odds that she doesn't. Jimmy's a crack addict. Wonder what crack's like. Probably fan-fucking-tastic. Damn. What the hell was I doing sitting there?

The meeting droned on with Joe's monotonous voice and monotone settling over me like a fog. Blah, blah, blah. I stole a look at my watch, hoping not to look rude and impatient, but wanting to know how much longer I had to endure the clichéd ramblings of a group facilitator who'd obviously been doing his job too many years. Five till twelve. Looked like I'd make it till lunch at least.

Finally, we were told to meet for CD Instruction after lunch. We finished the meeting with the Serenity Prayer.

On the way to the cafeteria Joe called me aside.

"Do you have one of these, Ali?" He held out a thick, blue, hardback book. "It's the AA Big Book."

"No."

"Take this. Read the first hundred pages tonight. And here's a

101

schedule of meetings. Find a meeting close to your house and make it your home group."

"Thanks." I offered my fake smile.

I stood in line for lunch. A couple of people from the previous day's group asked what had happened to me, where had I been. I explained about the insurance and how I was still in Unit Five, but was in a different group. We all sat together discussing music and family, and sharing addiction stories. Another normal everyday lunch with normal everyday addicts.

After lunch I went outside to a concrete bench in front of a bed of Impatiens, laid on my back and read. Others were walking around the track or standing in groups smoking. That was the one drug that seemed most common to the group, cigarettes. Guess everybody's allowed one addiction to cling to. I checked my watch. Time to get on with the second half of the day. Hope it wasn't going to suck as much as the first half.

When I walked into the community area two people were on the phones. There was a sign by each phone. Calls were only allowed at three set times during the day. Calls were not to exceed seven minutes in duration. Seven minutes? Who the hell came up with that magic number?

I wandered over to read the community rules posted on the wall. No radios were allowed, no headphones, no stereos, no cassette players, no compact disc players. No medicines at all; i.e. Ibuprofen, Aspirin, Hay Fever.

I walked into the ladies room. It was a mess. There weren't private bathrooms in the patient rooms, so all the women used one community bathroom. There were three blow dryers lying on the counter top, precariously close to the sinks and water. Combs, brushes, toothpaste and toothbrushes were scattered about. Women drifted in, bitching and griping about other female patients and all the rules, while I applied lipstick and ran a comb through my hair. Seemed I'd fallen into some sort of time warp and had suddenly been thrown back into high school. All the scene lacked was contraband cigarettes and drugs. I longed for a joint, anything that would get me high.

About twenty-five of us gathered in the CD Instruction room.

Glad I'd brought a sweater; they could've hung meat in there without so much as a second thought. Was there some edict that said addicts were always hot and must have plenty of cold air to survive, or were they trying to freeze us all to be thawed out later for scientific testing?

Shirley was our instructor for the day's lecture. First though, we were given the privilege of watching a lovely film about the effects drugs and alcohol have on the body. I had the pleasure to learn that a healthy liver weighs about three pounds, while an alcoholic's liver could actually weigh as much as fifteen pounds. It was quite a joy to learn that bit of biology immediately after eating.

After the film, and before anyone actually threw up, Shirley changed the subject. We then had the pleasure of discussing all the wonderful changes that would happen in our lives once we became healthy, non-abusing people. There was a veritable array of things to look forward to; better health, energy, hope, productive lives. All those things in contrast to the life of despair, fatigue, poor health, and deception we'd been leading.

"Is there anyone here that doesn't feel this way right now? That can't see this?"

I don't know quite what happened next. Maybe I'd spent too much time watching Adam, the speed freak, sleep, making bets with myself as to when someone would nudge him to wake him up, having to make adjustments to the timing if he started snoring, but I raised my hand. I was almost as surprised as the others in the room.

"Ali? You don't see this?"

"Well..." What the hell had I done? I'd spent the better part of the past week trying to be as inconspicuous as possible. "Well, I just don't feel like my life was really a mess to begin with. I haven't been feeling hopeless and desperate." I may as well have said that I went home every day and kicked my blind dog. The collective gasp wasn't audible, but I could feel it; almost a change in the barometric pressure of the room.

"How often were you getting high, Ali? Every day?"

"Yes."

"But you don't feel like your life was headed in the wrong direction?"

103

"No. Everything was pretty much fine." Ha, what a crock.

"No problems with your husband? You were getting everything done you needed to do every day? You were sleeping well and waking up feeling refreshed and ready for the day?"

"Sure." Now I was just being stubborn, but I'd gone too far to turn back. "No problems whatsoever." She saw right through me. Why did I think she hadn't heard that bullshit before.

"Ali, what are you going to do tonight?"

"I don't know. Probably work. I have a deadline I have to meet." More bullshit.

The rest of the room had fallen into silence. Shirley and I were the only ones staging this little two person performance, the others playing the part of the audience. No standing ovations for me today.

"I'm concerned about you, Ali. What are you going to do to keep from getting high this evening?"

"Don't know." I crossed my arms in front of my chest and crossed my legs. How predictable was that?

"Are you considering getting high tonight?"

"Sure. Considering that every night."

"Will you go to a meeting tonight?"

"Nope."

"Why not?"

"Busy."

"What can we do to help you?"

"Nothing. I'm fine."

We volleyed back and forth awhile before it was time for the meeting to end. I was the worse for wear and came out looking like a total ass. We all stood together and recited the Serenity Prayer.

After the meeting several people came up and expressed concern for me. Would I like to attend a meeting with them? Could they pick me up? Pretty nice, actually. But I wasn't interested.

Chapter 19

During the fourth day of Relapse Prevention Joe and I finally butted heads. I guess I knew from day one that it was going to happen. We'd never bonded.

Four of us were waiting for the others to arrive after lunch. We weren't having CD Instruction that day. Instead, we were going to continue the discussion we'd started in morning group – The Twelve Steps.

"So, Joe," I asked. "Are you an LPC?"

"No, an LCDC."

"What's an LPC?" someone in the room asked.

"A Licensed Professional Counselor," I answered smugly. "An LCDC is a Licensed Chemical Dependency Counselor," I added. I'd asked Alex about the qualifications needed for an LCDC. Evidently, in this state, you didn't have to be a licensed therapist to counsel the chemically dependent, nor did you have to have a college degree. Guess addicts and alcoholics weren't worthy of too much education and training.

I knew Joe was an addict himself, an alcoholic, to be exact. That's the way it worked. Recovering addicts showing the way for those who were beginning recovery.

"I never wanted to go the therapist route," Joe continued. "I just wanted to work with addicts."

And there he was, I thought, doing one hell of a lukewarm job.

"By the way, Ali, I require random UDS tests. After the meeting I want you to go to the front for testing."

Ah, the joys of recovery.

"Also, if you miss three days of meetings without permission, you're out."

When the others arrived Joe began the group. "Debbie, you want to start this afternoon? What step are you working on?"

"I'm working on step four, 'Made a searching and fearless moral inventory of ourselves.' I've started a list and I'm supposed to work with my sponsor when I leave here today. We're meeting at Denny's across the street."

"Great. That's good. Jake? What about you?"

"I'm on step three, turning my will and life over to God. This one's kinda hard for me. I've never been a religious person and this whole thing with God's kinda new to me. But I'm working on it. I've been praying and keeping an open mind. I think I finally do believe. So now I just have to Let Go and Let God."

"That's right," Joe said. "The third step is very important. As addicts, we're always wanting to be in control of everything. Wanting to say, 'Here, I can do that by myself,' or "I'm tough, I don't need anyone's help.' That kind of stinking thinking gets us into trouble. Because we can't do it all; not everything is in our control. What do you think, Heather?"

"Absolutely. I'm on the third step also, but I'm not really having any difficulty with it."

"That's good," Joe responded. "What about you, Ali? What step are you on?"

"Oh, well, I'm very religious so I don't have any problems working to turn my... uh, my..." I glanced up at the wall to read the poster where the Twelve Steps were listed. "To turn my will and life over to the care of God. I've practiced that every day for years."

"Okay. But what step are you on?"

"Well, I'm not really on any step. I haven't been working the steps."

He picked up the clipboard and thumbed through the sign-in sheets from the past four days. "I see you're not attending meetings. Is that correct?"

"Yes."

"So you don't have a sponsor, then?"

"That's right."

"When are you going to attend a meeting? There's a family meeting here at 7:30 tonight. Will you be there with your husband?"

I didn't tell him Alex shot pool on Thursdays and I wasn't about to ask him to forego that pleasure so he could sit around with a bunch of addicts. Besides, I had no intention of going myself.

"No."

"Why not?"

"I don't really care for AA. I've been exposed to it before; it's not for me. I don't like Twelve Step programs."

"The program works if you work the program, Ali."

STOP! I thought I'd throw up if I heard one more cliché. I smiled. "I know. I'm not saying it doesn't work. I'm just saying it's not for me."

You would've thought the air had been sucked out of the room by a huge vacuum. I'd committed a sacrilege.

"There's a place for every one in a Twelve Step program. I detect a bit of the rebel in you, Ali. Are you rebellious?"

"Yeah, I guess. I'll bet everyone in this room is a bit rebellious, though."

"I don't think you can speak in generalities like that," he said.

"Why not? That's what it's all about."

"Are you saying AA is about generalities?"

"Sure, just look at the signs hanging on your walls; Keep it Simple, First Things First."

"What are you doing here then, Ali?"

I folded my arms across my chest. "Beats me. My doctor made me come."

"Who's your doctor?"

"Ian McCain."

"I think we should get Dr. McCain on the phone."

"Fine. Let's do it," I said, stubborn as ever.

"If you're not going to cooperate, you're just wasting the group's time. Let's move on. I'll talk to you after the meeting."

"Whoa. Wait just a minute. I disagree that I'm wasting the group's time." I looked around at the others. "Is there anyone here who thinks I'm wasting their time?"

No one answered. They just sat there in silence.

"Carla, do you feel like I've been wasting your time these past four days?" I asked.

"No. I feel like you're somewhat negative, but, no, I wouldn't say you've wasted my time or the group's."

"Heather, what about you? Have I been wasting your time?"

"No, not at all."

"Jimmy?"

"No. Hell, I admire you for saying what you feel. And for staying so calm. Hell, if it was me I'd be telling Joe to go fuck himself. I'm amazed at how calm you are."

"Thank you. I..."

"Okay, let's continue." Joe interrupted. "We're almost out of time."

When the meeting ended we all stood in a circle holding hands.

"Ali, you want to close us out today?"

"Sure. Our Father, who art..."

Joe approached me as I stood in the hallway waiting for everyone to leave.

"Ali, why did Dr. McCain send you here?"

Oh, hell. Here we go again. I made sure to look him in the eye. "He thinks I smoke too much pot and take too many pills." Once again I didn't mention the drinking.

Joe then went on about how the whole program was based on the Twelve Steps and if I wasn't going to attend meetings then he didn't think he could do me much good. Thought he should call Dr. McCain and tell him that.

I agreed.

Chapter 20

As soon as I got into my car I turned on my cell phone. I called the dealer I used and stopped by his house to replenish the pot and pills I'd so recklessly thrown away. Since I'd also thrown out my pipe he gave me a few papers to see me through till I got to the store. He also had an assortment of pills to choose from. When I returned home I took the AA Big Book and schedule of meetings and tossed them in the trash. Good riddance.

There was a message from Joe saying he'd spoken with Dr. McCain. Joe strongly suggested I call Dr. McCain to reschedule my appointment for an earlier date. Great.

When Alex arrived home that night he told me he had to go to Indianapolis the following morning and would be gone for four days.

Free from the encumbrances of rehab and with Alex out of town, I spent the better part of the next four days stoned. I woke up in the mornings, took a shower, did a few things around the house, then rewarded myself with a couple of pills I'd carefully selected from my array, and lit a joint. When I achieved the high I was looking for, I listened to music until I fell asleep. When I woke up from my nap I got high again, enjoying the freedom of being completely alone with no concerns of anyone hassling me, and no concerns of drug testing. Screw AA, NA, MA, and all the other 'A's. In the evenings I broke out the vodka and continued my solitary party.

I didn't reply to any of my e-mail, and I didn't answer the phone when friends called. I wanted as little as possible to do with people.

Alex called each night to check on my day and tell me about his. I made a point not to be high between 6:30 and 8:00. I thought of things in advance to tell him that I'd done all day.

Even after Alex arrived home from his trip I stayed with my new schedule. When he called from work during the middle of the day I pretended I'd just woken up from a nap. When I wasn't asleep I was either listening to music or surfing the Web, looking for books. No matter what I tried I couldn't stop my own private porno films from playing in my mind.

I eventually had trouble finding the zone I was looking for and, desperate to maintain a suitable level of haze, I began to drink during the day to supplement my high. It still wasn't enough. I daydreamed about other drugs, wondered how I could get my hands on something new, maybe crack, and considered discussing it with my dealer. The munchies always won any contest of will power and I snacked on Tootsie Roll Pops, Jordan Almonds, and sesame seeds. Although I wasn't eating on a regular basis, preferring to get my calories through alcohol, I gained weight.

Alex was concerned and upset, but I didn't care. I continued to reassure him that I knew what I was doing, that I was in control.

The day of my dreaded appointment with Dr. McCain, I made sure my make-up, hair and clothes were exactly right. Didn't need any 'I told you so's' from him. I sat in my violet chair, listening to Alanis Morrisette through my headphones.

"Hi Ali. Come on in."

I walked ahead of Dr. McCain into his office and took my usual seat on his couch. He sat in his chair.

"So, Ali. You want to tell me what's going on?"

"Not much. You know."

"I understand you're no longer going to Whispering Pines."

"That's right."

"Are you getting high again?"

"Yes."

"Taking pills?"

"Yes."

"Drinking?"

"Yes." It was déjà vu. We'd had the same conversation only weeks before.

"How often are you getting high?"

I didn't answer. Just sat there trying to think of something clever to say, something to deflate the tension.

"Every day?"

"Yes."

"How much, Ali?"

I couldn't come up with an answer I liked and stupidly decided to go the brave, honest route. "Several times a day."

"I see. Are you drinking during the day as well?"

"Sure, figured I might as well go the whole nine yards."

He set his pad and pen in his lap, folded his hands over them and looked directly at me.

"Ali, I'm sorry, but I'm afraid I can't treat you anymore."

"What?" I was stunned.

"I told you before that I can't give you medication if you're going to continue to abuse drugs and alcohol. I won't be a party to your self-destruction."

"But..."

"Do you want to go into rehab? Check in for a twenty-eight day program?"

"God, no!"

"What are you going to do, then?"

"I don't know." Tears slid down my cheeks. All of a sudden I didn't feel so clever.

"You've got some decisions to make, Ali. Either you go through rehab, or you no longer receive treatment from me."

"Can't I just..."

"Those are your only two choices."

I sat there crying, not believing what he was telling me. I really liked him and didn't want to stop seeing him. I didn't want to give up the medicine that helped me sleep either. I jerked a tissue out of the box on the coffee table.

"But I don't like Twelve Step programs."

"Tough shit."

He waited for me to respond, but I was too busy crying.

"Did you stay clean while you were going to rehab?" he finally asked.

I didn't drink or get high if that's what you're trying to say, I thought to myself. "Yes," I answered.

"What are you going to do, Ali?"

"Oh, God. I don't know."

He continued to sit there, not moving a muscle, staring at me.

"I'll tell you what. Why don't you think about it? Go home, talk to your husband, get your priorities in order, and let me know what you decide." He stood up and opened the door.

"Okay."

"I really enjoy working with you, Ali. I hope you make the right decision."

"Thanks. Bye." I left his office, desperately trying to compose myself before I walked back out into the waiting room.

When I got home I made myself a drink and went straight to my stash. If there was ever a time when I was in need of a high, that was certainly it. When Alex opened the door to my office that evening I was startled. I hadn't even heard him come home. The afternoon had flown by with me sitting in my office listening to music and smoking.

There was a frown on his face when he walked in. He'd obviously smelled the pot and was visibly upset. "What're you doing?"

I knew he was pissed, but I couldn't think what to say. Finally, I just nonchalantly answered, "Oh, hi. You scared me. Did you just come in?"

"I've been here a minute. I looked for you in the bedroom first." He didn't mention the pot.

"Oh, sorry. Guess my headphones were kind of loud. How was your day?"

"Fine. Nothing exciting to report. How about yours?"

"I'll tell you over cocktails." He had no concerns about my drinking, being completely unaware of my little secret.

I followed him into the kitchen. When we finally sat down with our drinks, I was a bit nervous. I wasn't sure what kind of reaction I'd get from him in regards to the outcome of my visit with Dr. McCain. I never should have worried. He was calm and reassuring, but, in the end, agreed with Dr. McCain. I was a bit out of control.

"What are you going to do?" he asked. "You realize you have to make some significant changes?"

"Yeah, I know. I really don't want to think about that right now, though. That's all I've thought about since I left Dr. McCain's office. I'd prefer to hear about your day."

"Okay, but do you promise me you'll make some changes?"

"Yes, I promise. Cross my heart and hope to die." I stood up from the couch. "You want another drink?"

"Sure."

After mixing a rum and Coke for him and a vodka and 7 for me, I returned to the living room and handed him his fresh drink.

"Guess what?"

"What?"

"I bought you a present today."

"Where is it?" I glanced around his chair.

He reached behind him and grabbed my gift. "Here, it's in this bag." He handed me a Victoria's Secret bag and inside was a beautifully wrapped gift.

I opened it to discover a pair of white lace panties with a matching bra and garter belt. They were gorgeous, lacy and frilly. I jumped up and gave Alex a hug and kiss.

"Why don't you go try them on," he said.

I returned to the living room a short time later. Alex had lit some candles and opened a bottle of champagne! We had a fantastic evening, but after he fell asleep I was restless. I made myself another drink then went to my office, closed the door, and lit a joint.

Chapter 21

I resolved not to worry too much about Dr. McCain's ultimatum. I had enough medicine to last a month so there wasn't any real crisis. In the meantime, I could still see Eric.

On the morning of my appointment with Eric I jumped out of bed, took a shower, checked my e-mail, then got stoned. I listened to music and fell asleep on the living room floor with the headphones on. When I woke up, I put on my make-up, fixed my hair, dressed, mixed an extra strong drink, then left for Eric's office. I finished my vodka while sitting in the parking lot. When I got out of the car I strode to the elevator, not a care in the world. I pressed the button and waited. When the doors slid open I stepped in without a moment's hesitation. Can't believe I used to be afraid to ride in them.

I'd reached a pleasant state of drunkenness and was feeling pretty good by the time Eric came out for me.

"Hi, Ali. Looks like you're in your rebellious mood."

"Why do you say that?"

"The way you're dressed. Your black cap, your black boots."

"Ah, you know me better than I realized."

"What's going on with you?"

"Have you talked to Dr. McCain?" I asked.

"No, why?"

"Well, I hated rehab. Joe Mendoza was the Relapse Prevention counselor. Do you know him?"

"No."

"He's not very good. I kept wishing I was talking to you instead."

"Oh, so there are worse places than here?" He grinned.

"Yeah, hard to believe, eh? Anyway, Joe and I decided there wasn't any point in me continuing if I wasn't going to work the program, as they say. He called Dr. McCain and told him."

"I see."

"When I saw Dr. McCain last week, he asked if I was drinking, taking pills, and smoking again. When I said yes, he said he couldn't treat me anymore. Pretty much told me I had to decide what I was going to do about my life."

"And what are you going to do?"

"I don't know yet. Don't want to think about it right now."

"Was he right? Are you getting high a lot?"

"I guess that depends on whose definition we're using. If it's your definition, then the answer's probably yes. If it's mine, then I'd have to say no, not nearly enough. I feel like my whole life is a bit screwed up right now. I'm tired of always having to behave. I'm sick of it."

"That's an odd choice of words – having to behave. Is there anyone who tells you you're not behaving?"

"No. I just feel that way. Feel like I've always got to be doing the right thing. Don't worry; Ali will take care of it. No problem; ask Ali. Want a blow job; call Ali. Sorry."

"That's okay."

"God, I just hate it!"

"How much have you had to drink, Ali?"

"Damnit. Does it always have to be about alcohol and drugs and sex?"

"I only asked about the alcohol. You're obviously drunk."

"Oh, crap. Yeah. I'd rather be high. But I think the state frowns on smoking pot and driving. I considered bringing a joint anyway. I'm in the good car, though, and Alex would have a cow if I smoked pot in it. Don't think you can get that Marijuana smell out very easily." I leaned back on the couch with my eyes closed.

"How much have you had to drink Ali?"

"I don't know. Obviously not enough."

"How are you going to get home?"

"I'll be okay by then."

"No, I won't let you drive. Who can you call?"

"I'll call Matt to see if he can pick me up. He only lives about three miles from here. Good ol' Matt. Bless him. Always call him when I need to talk. At least if it's stuff I can't talk to Alex about."

"What kind of things are you unable to discuss with Alex?"

"Oh, nothing. I can discuss about anything with him really. Except my drug use. He's sick to death of it. And my alcohol use, of course. He doesn't know I'm drinking during the day. He'd be upset if he knew I came here drunk today. But Matt won't say much, even though he'll probably be upset, too."

"Why do you think they'll be upset?"

I stood up and walked around the office. "They profess to care about me. And my behavior worries them."

"You don't believe they really care about you?"

"Oh yeah. I'm sure they do. I just get tired of feeling like I have to be good. Why can't I just say 'fuck everyone' and do what I damn well please?"

"You can. But there'd be consequences."

"I know. I don't really want to do that. Wait, that's not true, part of me does. And part of me wants to be the perfect wife. I'm sorry, I'm rambling."

"How do you see the perfect wife?"

"A woman who always looks exactly right; hair, make-up, clothes. All that crap. Someone who cooks perfect dinners every night and waits on her husband hand and foot. Takes care of him after his long day at the office. I guess something right out of *Happy Days*. Someone who pleases her man. Ha. Someone different from me."

"You don't think you're a good wife?"

"Yeah, I really do – overall. But I go through bouts of being horrible. Don't know why Alex continues to put up with me. I do try. To please him, that is."

"You think that's important?"

"Sure. At least that's what I've been taught since I was a kid. Please the man. Yuck. Don't like the way that sounds."

"Why not?"

I stopped walking, sat down again and leaned back on the couch, my arms spread across the back. "I don't know. When I hear that, it makes me think of sex."

"Why is that do you think?"

"Don't know. Just does. When I hear the phrase 'please the man' I immediately get a picture of me on my knees – figuratively and literally."

"So pleasing a man always involves sex?"

"Yep. At least the way I learned it. That's what everything always comes down to – sex."

"You've said your cousin started having sex with you when you were eleven. Right?"

"Yep. Nothing like keeping it in the family."

"And you started performing oral sex on him a year later?"

"Yeah, guess he didn't know about that little pleasure till then. He sure as hell wouldn't have waited so long."

"What about Jack? Did you perform oral sex on him?"

I stood up again and walked to the window. "Oh, yeah. Didn't want to miss anyone. I woulda been a helluva lot of fun at family reunions, eh? I'm telling you, that's what I was trained for – my whole life. I'm damned good. Too bad it's not an Olympic sport. I was twelve by the time Jack worked his way up to actually screwing me. Of course, Scott had been screwing me for a year by then, so it wasn't like it was a big deal. In fact, I remember the first time Jack screwed me. It was at night and I was in bed, of course. I was lying there, almost waiting for him. It's weird now to think about it, but I learned his pattern. Knew when he'd be in. I don't know what it was or how I knew. I just did. Anyway, after he came in and locked the door, I immediately got undressed. He didn't haveta say a word. That was the routine that had developed. He usually stood in front of me or sat on my bed with his pants unzipped and me, you know, doing my part. This time, though, he took his pants completely off. I knew then what was next. He told me to lie back down on the bed. Then he got on top of me."

I still hadn't turned around to look at Eric. I was embarrassed and ashamed. I continued with my monologue.

"When he put it in me I remember letting out a cry. He was so much bigger than Scott and I wasn't ready, you know, and it hurt. When I hollered, he put his hand over my mouth and told me to be quiet. Told me I'd get in trouble if anyone ever found out and that I had to mind him and behave."

"And you never told anyone then?"

"Hell no. Who was I going to tell?"

"But you have told Alex?"

"Oh yeah. Told him before we got married. When we got serious. You see, well, when Alex and I finally ended up going to bed, I was pretty weird."

"What do you mean?"

I began pacing. "You know. I didn't realize the woman was supposed to actually enjoy the procedure. Yuck, that sounds clinical. I mean the process. Oh hell, whatever you want to call it. I thought it was the woman's job to keep quiet and just do as she was told. Please the man."

"And?"

"And Alex actually took time for me, to make sure I was enjoying it. I thought 'this poor guy doesn't know how it's supposed to work.' I couldn't believe it. I think that's when I fell in love with him. He was so gentle, unselfish, caring. It was a revelation to me; sex could actually be lovemaking. Wow, what a thought."

"And now?"

I turned to look at him. "What do you mean?"

"How is it now – sex?"

"Well, it's fine. Why?"

"No reason. Just asking."

"It's fine, great." I took up my post at the window again. "You know I really hate talking about sex. Let's change the subject. Did you have a good week-end?"

"Boy, you're not even subtle."

"Nah. No point in it. Besides, it's time for me to leave."

Chapter 22

Over the next two weeks I began to feel quite smug. I was smoking, taking pills, and drinking as much as I liked, fantasizing about crack and heroin, and not missing Dr. McCain's services too much. Alex was concerned, but I continued to tell him that it was a phase; that I was in therapy, at least, and not to worry.

The waiting room was full of parents and children when I walked in for my next appointment with Eric. Must be coming up on a full moon. I knew Eric and Dr. McCain worked with children quite a bit, but I'd never given it much thought. Seeing so many of them in the office, though, was heartbreaking. Wonder what could've possibly happened in their young lives that they were already in need of therapy. How sad. I hated to think that some of them might be sexually abused. But maybe seeing them there wasn't so sad after all. Maybe it was a good thing. Maybe I wouldn't be so screwed up if I would've told; if I would've had help when I was younger instead of spending years trying to pretend it never happened.

I listened to my music while I studied the kids. Every once in awhile I made eye contact with one of them and gave them a wink and a smile. I had a tremendous desire to jump up and wrap each one of them in a hug. One little boy in particular looked painfully shy. How could anyone hurt someone so trusting and naïve? I leaned my head back and closed my eyes. Didn't want to become too caught up in the kids. They seemed too fragile.

For only the second time since I'd begun seeing Eric, he kept me waiting. Fifteen minutes after the hour he called me in.

"Hi Ali."

"Hi. Boy, there are a lot of people here today."

"Yeah, pretty busy."

I sat down on the couch. Eric took his usual seat diagonally across. This time, though, he leaned toward me and began talking immediately.

"Ali, I've decided I can't see you anymore if you're going to continue to drink and use drugs."

"What?" I stared at him.

"Right now, Ali, your primary problem is drug abuse. The sexual abuse has become secondary. Until you deal with the drug problem you won't be able to deal with anything else. Therapy isn't helping you."

I sat there, stunned, not uttering a word.

"I'm sorry," he said. "But my ethics won't allow me to continue when I know I'm not helping you. We're just spinning our wheels."

I started crying. "But I'll do better. I know I can."

"Good. I certainly hope so. But until you show me that you can, I have to stop seeing you. I've discussed it with Dr. McCain and we both agree on this."

"Did you tell him I was drunk last week when I came?"

"Yes."

"Damnit."

"He said you've been high a couple of times during your meetings with him."

"Oh, hell. I don't remember."

"I'll tell you what. I won't charge you for today. Why don't you take the week and decide what you're going to do. I'll see you here next week and you can let me know your decision. You really have to give this some careful consideration."

"I know. Will Dr. McCain make me go back to rehab?"

"I don't know. I can't speak for him."

"Oh, damn." Tears rolled down my cheeks.

"I'm sorry to have to do this, Ali, but it's for your own good."

"I know."

He stood up. "See you next week then?"

"Okay." I grabbed a tissue from the box and left.

I considered going straight home and getting high, but called Matt instead. His answering machine picked up.

"Hi, it's me. I was just wondering if you were home. I really need to talk. I know you're busy tonight, but I thought if you had twenty minutes, maybe I could drop by. Why don't you give me a call on my cell phone if you get this within the next half hour? Maybe I'll go to the bookstore."

As soon as I walked into the bookstore, Matt called. I walked back outside and sat in my car talking.

"What's wrong?" he asked. "How was your session with Eric?"

"Not too good."

"Oh, why not?"

"He won't see me anymore until I deal with the drug thing."

"Well, surely you saw that coming, Ali."

"No, I really didn't. I didn't think he'd turn on me, too."

"Ali, come on. You expect me to believe that?"

"Yeah."

He chuckled. "You want to come over?"

"When do you have to leave for the play?"

"In about half an hour."

"No, then, that's alright. I'm not that close. I'm at the bookstore on Cullen. Thanks, though. I'll be okay."

"Ali, you've been trying to deal with the drug problem and the abuse for years. What made you think Eric was going to let you get away with it?"

"I don't know. It's only pot and some pain pills, or Xanax, or whatever. Besides, I just don't think it's as bad as everyone keeps making it out to be."

"Yeah, right."

"Really, I swear!"

"Well, it's time for you to finally do something. Or I guess you could cope the same way you've been coping. Use drugs and grow into a little old lady who never resolves the sexual abuse problem. That's one alternative to getting clean and continuing your therapy."

Oh great. Now Matt was using the ridiculous jargon.

I started crying again. "I don't know what to do," I answered.

"Surely you're joking."

"No. I mean it."

"You have to give up the drugs and alcohol."

"But I don't want to. I just don't see why I can't keep getting high and still see Eric. Maybe I'll just quit going to therapy."

"You're not seriously considering that as an option, are you?"

"Yes, kind of."

"Please. That's absurd."

"I'm not sure why I started going to begin with."

"Let's see, because you were constantly frightened, unhappy and

123

depressed? Having nightmares nearly every night!"

"Oh yeah."

"Ali, you've made a lot of progress. How could you even consider quitting? That'd be like going to college and quitting the last semester before you earned your degree. You know what you have to do."

"I know. I just don't want to. I like being high."

"Yeah, it's easier than dealing with the real problem."

"I'll let you go," I said. "I think I'll hang out here awhile before I go home. Tonight's Alex's pool night."

"So, you're going to go home and get high, right?"

"Yeah, thought I would."

"Why don't you go with me? Someone in our group cancelled and I have an extra ticket."

"No, thanks. I just want to go home.

"You sure? You're more than welcome."

"No, I appreciate it, but I really want to be home."

"Okay. Call me if you change your mind."

"I will. Thanks for listening."

"No problem. Any time."

I hung up the phone and sat in my car crying. Screw the bookstore. I started the car and headed for home, fantasizing about ways to hurt Jack and Scott.

Chapter 23

When I arrived home, I sat at my desk tearing Marijuana pieces away from the compressed ounce and pulling stems out. After I'd prepared enough to roll a joint I remembered I didn't have any papers left. And I still hadn't replaced my pipe. Damn.

I drank a vodka and 7-Up, took a couple of Darvocet, and sat in my office while I figured out what to do, angry at myself for not remembering to stop at the head shop on my way home. I finally pulled a pack of sticky notes from my desk drawer and rolled a joint. It was a bit cumbersome, but it worked.

By the time Alex walked in from work that evening I'd taken a quick shower, fixed my make-up after crying half of it off, and straightened up around the house. I kept thinking I really needed to pull myself together, but Alex was shooting pool that night so I decided I might as well spend the evening smoking and drinking. After all, I couldn't be expected to stop immediately. I'd already gotten high that morning and afternoon, so the day was already used, so to speak. I'd start my new program tomorrow.

Once again I dreaded telling Alex about my visit with Eric. I didn't have to mention it at all, but I knew he'd ask. When I heard the car, I stepped outside.

"Hi darling."

"Hi. You look nice," he said.

"Oh, thanks." I took his briefcase from him while he gathered his dry cleaning from the back seat. "You have a good day?"

"Yes, how about you?"

"Pretty good," I answered.

"How was your visit with Eric?"

"Not too good." I followed him into the bedroom and lay on the bed while he hung up his shirts.

"Why not?"

I told him the whole story then, even confessing to him about my daily drinking and all the pills I'd been taking. I cried uncontrollably. Where in the hell were all these tears coming from? Was it possible that I'd eventually use my allotted amount and never cry again?

125

"I'll tell you what," Alex said. "How about I skip pool tonight and you and I go out for a nice dinner?"

"That'd be great! Are you sure?"

"Yeah, I think you need some company tonight."

"Thanks, honey."

"I'll call Ben and tell him. Why don't you get dressed up? We'll go to Prego."

"Okay!" I jumped up from the bed and hurried to change clothes.

We had a fantastic meal, lingering over every course while we talked. I couldn't believe Alex was being so supportive. Don't know what I ever did to deserve him, but I thanked God every day for sharing him with me.

After we returned home we spent two hours in bed, laughing, playing, and making love. I decided life couldn't get much better. While Alex slept I lay in the bed, tossing, turning, and thinking about my session with Eric. I couldn't get it off my mind. An hour and a half later I was still wide awake. I just couldn't turn my brain off.

Finally, I gave up, got out of bed, put some clothes on, and went into the kitchen. I made myself a drink and went into my office where I rolled another joint with my sticky notes.

My next appointment with Eric was scheduled for the following Wednesday. I decided I had through Tuesday night to continue getting high and drinking and that I'd begin my new drug free sober lifestyle on Wednesday.

I was stoned when the phone rang the next morning. When I saw it was the office I didn't bother to answer. They left a message, letting me know there was work that needed to be finished as soon as possible. I thought about blowing it off, but decided I could work while I was stoned. It certainly didn't take a mental giant to type names, addresses, and numbers into a computer. I put on my headphones, smoked another joint, and worked. It was a breeze. Why had I waited so long to try it? Work would never be the same! Except I was supposed to quit smoking and drinking. Oh, well. Plenty of time to worry about that next week.

I spent the week stoned and drunk, not bothering to cook, clean house, answer the phone, or talk to friends. Alex was extremely upset by my behavior, but I didn't care. I told him not to worry, that

I'd be a different person beginning Wednesday.

The night before my appointment with Eric I sat up till 4:00 a.m. getting totally wasted. I figured it was my last hurrah, so to speak, and I might as well go out with a bang. At 8:00 the next morning I woke up vomiting. I took an Imitrex for my migraine, got a cold washcloth for my head and went back to bed. I was glad Alex had already left for work. I couldn't sleep and when my headache subsided I got up and wandered around the house aimlessly. I was still sick to my stomach and my hands shook. I tried to eat, but couldn't keep anything down. When the anxiety was more than I could bear, I lit a joint and made myself a drink. I felt better immediately. Maybe I'd made the wrong decision to give up the drugs and alcohol and continue with my therapy. How was I ever going to make it through a whole day without my vodka, pills, and pot? I fell asleep on the floor while listening to *Matchbox 20*.

When I woke up from my nap I felt pretty good. I took my time getting dressed for my appointment. As I drove to Eric's office I tried to imagine a drug free life. What the hell was I thinking? Why was I doing this? Maybe I should turn around, call Eric's office from my cell phone and cancel my appointment; leave a message that I didn't think I needed therapy after all. But I kept driving while I gave myself little pep talks. You can do it, Ali. You can do anything you set your mind to. All you have to do is dig your heels in. Just keep it simple and take it one day at a time. Oh, hell, now I was spouting Twelve Step crap.

When Eric called me into his office I was a complete wreck; shaky and anxious.

"So how are you feeling, Ali?"

The lie fell from my lips automatically. "Fine. Great." I took my regular seat on the couch.

"I assume you've made some decisions?"

"Well, maybe. But I have a few questions."

"Okay, that's fair."

"What are the ground rules?" I asked. "Are you saying no drugs or alcohol at all?

"That's right."

"Will you believe me?"

127

"I think so. You've been pretty honest with me. You don't hide it as well as you think anyway. How about you promise to stay clean and sober and I'll take your word for it. Unless, of course, your behavior causes me to be suspicious. If that happens I'll want a UDS."

"Okay. I'll agree to that."

"I'm not saying it's going to be easy, Ali. The therapy's going to be rough. There'll be times when you'll want to get high, but you can't. You've got to see this through if you're going to grow."

"I know."

"And I'm not saying you won't be using a month from now."

Using. I was sick to death of the word.

"You always have the option of discontinuing therapy and going back to the drugs. You just can't have it both ways. But if you do that, you won't get any better. You still won't have dealt with the sexual abuse."

I sat there, barely moving, feeling like I'd entered some sort of parallel universe and that it wasn't really me he was talking to.

"You willing to try it?"

"Okay. I guess so."

"That's great. I know you can do this. You're intelligent and strong and I know you want to feel better."

"Yeah, I really do. Have you talked to Dr. McCain yet? Is he going to make me go back to rehab?"

"I don't know. You'll have to see what he says. I only talked to him briefly before he left for vacation."

"God, I hope not. I don't know if I can do that."

"Have you discussed any of this with Alex?"

"Yes, he's been pretty upset with me. He was really happy when I told him I'd probably do this."

"When's the last time you got high, Ali? Today?"

"Yes." Damn. How did he know that?

"You understand that's it then? That today's your last day?"

"Yes."

"Okay. How about you come in next week and we'll get started?"

"That sounds good."

When I got home I made myself a drink, took a couple of Xanax, and lit a joint. The way I figured it, I couldn't count today anyway so I might as well make the best of it. One last night of partying while Alex was out having a beer with a friend. I'd start tomorrow.

Chapter 24

The day after my appointment with Eric I woke up with a hangover. Oh well. That wouldn't be a problem anymore. It was my first chemical free day. This time I didn't have to throw away any of my pot or pills. I'd used up everything. Eric had told me I wouldn't be able to pass a UDS for three to four weeks, and, contrary to popular belief, there was withdrawal from Marijuana. The psychological effects would be noticeable immediately. I wouldn't begin to experience any physical effects for about a month. "However," he said, "You'll probably start feeling the withdrawal from all the pills and alcohol within the next few days."

The day went by pretty quickly with me working several hours, then vacuuming, cleaning bathrooms, mopping floors, and washing clothes. I was a woman possessed. When Alex arrived home we went out to our favorite Mexican restaurant for dinner. Neither Alex nor I had any drinks with our meal. After dinner we watched some television, then went to bed. I read awhile before falling asleep. I'd made it through day one. No big deal.

Since I'd made the decision to try this little experiment of clean living I called to make an appointment with Dr. McCain to see if he'd agree to meet with me and refill my prescriptions. I was almost out of the medicine I took at night to help me sleep and that was a pill I desperately needed if I was going to stay away from alcohol and all the other stuff. Unfortunately, Dr. McCain was still on vacation and was already booked for the first week of his return. I wasn't able to schedule an appointment for three weeks, which caused a bit of a panic in me. I'd been so smug when I had a lot of medicine, but now I was scared.

The second day of my new life wasn't quite as easy. I cleaned out the refrigerator, gave the kitchen a scrubbing from top to bottom, changed the linen on the bed, paid bills, then paced the floors. Looked like it was going to be a long-ass day. While Alex and I watched a movie on television that night, I labeled pictures and put them into a photo album. I drank copious amounts of iced tea and complained about how much I hated my new lifestyle. Why the hell had I agreed to such a ridiculous scheme? After all, they were only minor drugs. For the hundredth time I told myself that it wasn't serious; it wasn't like I was taking PCP or shooting heroin. What was the big deal? Why was everyone so concerned?

I woke up bright and early Saturday morning bursting with energy. Alex and I went to the grocery store, to the post office, and to other mundane places to perform boring petty chores. When we got home I balanced the bank statement, then cleaned both bathrooms again. I thought I was going to scream. God, if I could just have a couple of hits I'd feel better; even just one drink or maybe a couple of Xanax. Maybe this whole thing wasn't such a good idea. I scrounged around to see if I had any pot or pills at all – something I may have previously overlooked. I didn't need much; just a little something. No such luck. I'd done a good job of smoking and swallowing everything in sight.

Matt came over for dinner that night. I wasn't exactly the Martha Stewart of hostesses. I spent the majority of the evening being a pain in the ass; constantly repeating, "I hate this, I hate this, I hate this." Alex and Matt were both patient and encouraging, telling me it was best this way, that it was about time I dealt with my problems instead of finding ways to stay numb. Easy talk for people who didn't have a damn clue what I was feeling.

Sunday morning I dropped Alex off at the pool hall to practice, then went to two bookstores. I spent hours trying to lose myself in the books, trying to generate some enthusiasm. It didn't work. When I returned to pick up Alex, I sat for awhile and watched him shoot pool. After we arrived home I dusted and polished the furniture, entered books into my database, and surfed the web for first editions. We decided to go to the movies. I ate a bucket of popcorn while I squirmed in my seat. When we returned home Alex went straight to bed. At 2:00 a.m. I finally gave in to the fear and anxiety rattling around my body and went to bed myself. I was exhausted. I lay there crying until 4:00 when I finally fell asleep. I'd made it through my fourth day – barely.

At 8:00 a.m. I was wide awake. Damn. Another day from hell. The instructors at rehab liked to remind us that lack of sleep never killed anyone. I was beginning to seriously question the validity of their data. After working four hours I had nothing left to do. I considered removing all the dishes and cleaning out the cabinets, but decided in the end to go to another bookstore. That helped immensely. On the way home I stopped at the grocery store to pick up supplies for an elaborate dinner. After dinner, we cleaned the kitchen, then watched television while I worked on photo albums some more. I felt like screaming. I finally forced myself to go to bed at 3:00 a.m. After tossing and turning for an hour and a half, I fell asleep. Day five sucked.

On the sixth day I woke up at 8:00 a.m. again. I couldn't believe how exhausted I was, but how little I was sleeping. What was I going to do with another day facing me full in the face? After wandering around the house, I spent the morning writing hateful fake letters to Jack and Scott, telling them I wished they both ended up in prison, gang raped by a group of very large, mean men. My anger spent, I lay on the floor listening to music and crying. Fatigue finally got the better of me and I fell asleep. When I woke up I worked for four hours, then tried in vain to find some way to amuse myself. I thought about cooking another elaborate dinner, but didn't really care if Alex or I ever ate again. Screw him. He could feed himself. I sat in my office that evening surfing the web and writing in my journal. I was in no mood to be around anyone; not even Alex. I had an appointment with Eric for the next afternoon. I felt like it would help immensely to talk to him and figured everything would be okay if I could just make it through one more night. I couldn't believe I was having such a difficult time with the whole thing. After all, I continued to tell myself, it was only alcohol and Marijuana and an occasional pill. No big deal. But damn, I needed a drink or a joint, preferably both.

Much to my surprise, I lived through the week. Alex and the few friends who knew about my secret life were very proud of me. I, on the other hand, wanted to strangle everyone I came into contact with. Because Alex had a late appointment that evening, Matt and I decided to go out for a bite to eat after my session with Eric; to celebrate my week of clean living, Matt said.

As I dressed and prepared to leave the house for my appointment, I had an overwhelming desire to mix myself a drink for the road. I went so far as to take the vodka out of the cupboard. I set the bottle on the counter, then stood there staring at it. I slowly screwed off the cap and held it to my nose like it was some fine wine and I was enjoying the pleasant, robust bouquet of the Smirnoff. Finally, through sheer will power, I returned it to the cupboard. I arrived at Eric's office clean and sober, as everyone insisted on labeling it. I sat in my violet chair in the waiting room listening to Pavarotti, trying to soothe the savage breast, as they say. I felt like I was going to throw up. I walked ahead of Eric into his office.

"How're you doing, Ali?"

"Okay, I guess. Not great." I took a seat on the couch.

"Tell me what's going on."

"It's been a week since I've had any alcohol or anything else and so far I hate it."

"That's great that you've made it through the week. But it's not going to be easy. You knew that. If it were easy, it wouldn't be called addiction."

"I know. I just really, really hate it, though. Last night I even dreamed about getting high. Dreamed about shooting speed, which is really weird because I've never done any IV drugs."

"That's not uncommon among addicts, Ali. They often dream of using after they've quit. You'd know that if you went to some of the so called stupid meetings."

Damn. There was that ridiculous word again. Addict. Why was everyone so hung up on labels? And wrong ones, at that. I smiled at him, but didn't respond.

"What does Alex have to say about all this?"

"I didn't tell him about my dream. He wouldn't understand. He's excited I'm not spending my days and nights getting wasted. But there are other problems now."

"Like what?"

"Well... The other night he wanted to make love and I told him I couldn't unless I was stoned or drunk. He wasn't too happy to hear that."

"Why do you think that is?"

"That he wasn't happy?"

"No, that you have to be stoned or drunk?"

"Oh. I don't know." I picked up my headphones and fidgeted with the cord. "I just feel like when I'm having sex that I'm performing. And if I'm stoned or drunk, then I can go someplace else. In my mind, I mean. That's what I always did with Jack and Scott and the others – just go someplace else."

"Why do you think that bothers Alex?"

I stood up and walked around. "Damn, I promised myself I wasn't going to cry today." I grabbed a tissue and sat back down in a chair on the other side of the room. "He said if I'm high, that it wasn't the same. That it wasn't really me he was making love to. God, I hate talking about this."

"You think he's interested in you then and not just the sex?"

"Yeah, weird, huh? I think he actually wants to have sex as an expression of love. I don't know how to do that."

"I'm not surprised. You've been trained otherwise. You've never had sex with anyone who loved you, have you? Except Alex."

"Yeah. Guys said they loved me, of course. But I wasn't so stupid as to believe them. It really pissed me off, in fact. Insulted my intelligence. God, I really hate men."

"Do you believe Alex loves you?"

"Yeah, I guess. Sure. I don't understand why, though. It still surprises me."

"Do you like for him to touch you, hold you?"

"Oh God, yes. That's wonderful. I love it when he just puts his arm around me and pulls me up against him."

"But when it starts getting physical you have problems?"

I stood up and paced the floor. "Yeah. I don't know why he cares so much if I get high first. I can do any manner of things if I'm high. At least he's getting laid. Seems to me it works out pretty well for all concerned."

"Maybe he's not interested in you doing any manner of things. Or in just getting laid. He loves you. He wants a relationship. You think he stayed with you these past years just for the great sex?"

I chuckled. "No. But I just need to be able to go someplace else in my mind. Get away from it."

"You know, Ali, you're really fortunate. Most people who've been through what you have don't end up as well off as you. They

135

often end up in an abusive relationship. They have serious problems; multiple personality disorder, schizophrenia, bipolar disorder, any number of things."

"I know. I've really been blessed." I sat back down on the couch. "Oh, hell. I don't know what to do."

Eric leaned forward, his hands clasped together. "Why don't you tell Alex how you feel? See if you can take things slowly?"

"Yeah, maybe. I don't know." I started crying again. "I just want to get high, damnit."

He smiled at me. "Yes, you've said that."

When I left Eric's office I called Matt to see if he was home from work yet so we could go to dinner to celebrate my one week. When he didn't answer I left a message on his machine and sat in his parking lot waiting for him to call me back on my cell phone. After an hour I gave up and went to a bar. I had four drinks before I heard from him. He was finally home. He was sorry for being late, he said, but he'd been in a meeting all afternoon and it had lasted longer than expected. If I wanted to come on over he'd be ready to go out shortly. I didn't tell him I was at a bar.

As soon as I walked into his apartment I asked for a drink. He told me he didn't have any liquor, but I knew better. I'd bought some vodka a couple of months earlier to keep there, just for such an occasion. He refused to show me where it was, but I searched through his cupboards until I found it. I made myself a drink while he stood in the doorway of the kitchen expressing his disappointment. I didn't care. When I walked past him into the living room, he told me I reeked of alcohol. I didn't care about that either. I was just happy to have a drink in my hand. I lay on the floor and sipped my vodka and 7 while he changed for dinner. He told me he'd go with me to get something to eat, but that we obviously couldn't celebrate a week of me being clean and sober. And again, I didn't care. I was quite pleasantly drunk.

When we arrived at the restaurant I staggered to our table and ordered a drink. All through dinner he continued to tell me how unhappy he was with my behavior and I continued to ignore him. It wasn't a big deal. Tomorrow was another day, after all. I'd just start on the sober part of my new life then. At least I wasn't getting high.

After eating we went back to his apartment. He sat in a chair while I laid on the floor whining. When he thought I was sober enough to drive I left, but had to promise to call him when I arrived home. He told me if I didn't take the remaining vodka home with me he was going to pour it down the sink. He refused to play any part in my destruction. Of course I wouldn't allow him to commit the sin of dumping perfectly good alcohol, so I bundled it up and carefully carried it to my car. When I arrived home I was glad to see Alex was still out. I walked in the door, set down the vodka, and went straight to bed. I was already beginning to experience the after affects of my little binge.

Chapter 25

The week crawled by. I was constantly on edge and depressed. Instead of being filled with restless energy as the week before, I was now exhausted. I stumbled out of bed each morning dreading the hours of the coming day. After I finished the few hours of work I had, I lay on the floor listening to music and fantasizing about drugs and being high and trying to remember more specific incidents of the abuse. I had it in my head that if I could recall each and every occurrence, then I could deal with it, put it completely behind me, and move on to the next occurrence. And, one by one, I would have finally dealt with it all and put the demons to rest.

When friends asked us to join them for dinner I made up excuses why we couldn't go. The very thought of food made me want to gag and I was in no mood to be around anyone anyway. I knew our friends were concerned, but they didn't understand. I couldn't be bothered to discuss such mundane topics as movies, books, vacations, or anything that wasn't in some way related to drugs or abuse.

At night I sat in my office and cried. What the hell had I agreed to? I thought about how much I enjoyed downers and wondered where I could get my hands on some really powerful ones. I continued to wonder what it would be like to try heroin – just once. Too bad I hadn't asked Grace, the heroin addict in rehab, for her phone number. I'll bet she wasn't lying around fantasizing about being high. She was probably out there enjoying it – if she wasn't dead.

I finally took the last pill Dr. McCain had prescribed to help me sleep. My appointment with him wasn't for another ten days. How the hell did he expect me to go to bed at night without my medicine? What kind of uncaring person would place me in such a situation? When I first met him I honestly believed he really cared about me. It was plainly evident to me now that he was just a cold and heartless bastard. Another man.

After working six hours the next day I sat on the couch searching for something decent to watch on television, anything for a distraction. As I chewed my ham sandwich, which was devoid of any flavor, I began to have trouble breathing. My hands were clammy and my heart raced. I became frightened that I couldn't breathe, which only resulted in my breathing becoming more shallow. I sat there, terrified, sucking in air in shallow gasps. Sitting up seemed to make it worse, so I dropped my sandwich onto the plate and hurriedly got down on the floor. It didn't help. I broke out into a sweat. When I finally recognized the fact that I was having an anxiety attack, I began to give myself reassurances; calm down, Ali; breathe slowly and deeply; calm and relaxed. I inhaled through my nose and exhaled through my mouth, all the time trying to remember the self hypnosis techniques Alex had taught me so long ago. I stretched out, my arms and legs extended, hands open. I closed my eyes and imagined myself at the beach, calm and relaxed. I could hear the surf pounding against the shore; serene and peaceful. I could hear the seagulls squawking overhead; breathe slowly and deeply. I could smell the salt air and feel the sand against my skin; breathe and relax. After what seemed like a lifetime, I was breathing normally again. I continued to lie there, tears slipping from my eyes. Please God, don't let this happen again. I don't think I can do this. Please just let me get high one more time. Why? Why? Why was I doing this?

When Alex arrived home I was on the verge of tears. I wanted to find an open field, stand in the middle of it, and scream until my throat bled.

Lying in bed that night I pulled one of the oldest tricks in the book. I waited until Alex was asleep to begin a conversation I should have started four hours earlier, after dinner.

"Alex," I said, nudging him, "I need to talk to you."

"Uh-huh." He stirred a bit. "What is it?"

"Can you turn over? I really need to talk."

"Oh, Ali. Can't it wait? I'm really tired."

"Sure. Never mind. Sorry to bother you," I said hatefully. I couldn't believe the selfish, whining bitch I'd become. I rolled away from him.

He turned toward me. "That's okay. What's so important?"

"Nothing. I'll talk to you later." I moved as close as I could to my side of the bed without actually falling off.

"Sweetheart, what is it?"

"It's not that important. Go to sleep."

"Come on, Ali." He reached over and touched my shoulder. "Don't do this. What do you want?"

I turned to face him. "I'm sorry, honey. I just really need to talk to someone."

He lay there, leaning on his elbow, his head propped up on his hand. "Okay. What about? Talk to me."

"Well, I don't know."

"Ali, dang it. I was asleep and now you're saying you woke me up to tell me you don't know what you wanted to talk about?"

"I'm sorry. It's just that, well, I don't think I want to continue going to therapy. I think I want to start getting high again."

"Oh, God. That's what this is all about?" He sat up in the bed.

"Yeah."

"Please tell me you're joking."

"No. I mean it. I don't see that anything's better since I've stopped."

"Hell, Ali, it's only been ten days!"

"I know. But I can't stand it. I just want to smoke a little sometimes. What's the big deal? It's only pot."

"That's like someone saying they're not an alcoholic because they only drink beer. You know better than that. You know how it affects you; how it changes everything about you. It doesn't matter what the drug is. It's still a drug."

"Well..."

"And now you're saying you want to stop going to therapy?"

"Yeah, well, you know, Eric won't see me if I'm smoking and drinking."

"Oh, so you're going to start drinking again, too?"

"Not a lot. Just sometimes." I finally gave in to the misguided jargon. "I don't like being clean and sober all the time. I really hate it. I wouldn't do it much, I swear."

He jumped up from the bed and swung around to face me. "Ali, do you have any idea what I'm going through? Do you even care what you're doing to me?"

"Of course." I sat up.

"You don't even know, do you? Every day I listen to people with problems. All day. And I'm doing my very best to try to help them. Then when I get home, the house and you and everything else smells like pot and you're stoned and drunk." He ran his hand through his hair.

"I'm sorry. I..."

"Hush. Just wait a minute. I'm trying to help people all day and I can't even help my own wife! I worry about you constantly. Did you know that?"

"No," I whispered.

"Well, I do. And I feel like I'm doing an injustice to my own clients because I'm spending so much time worried about you. I don't know if I'm going to come home one day and find you lying on the floor dead or..."

"Dead? That's ridiculous."

"No it's not. I know you, Ali. One drug isn't enough for you. Have you started smoking crack yet?"

"Of course not. How ludicrous."

"Don't tell me the thought hasn't crossed your mind, that you're not trying to figure out some way to find a better high. Admit it, Ali. I know you used to talk about trying heroin. Been thinking about that again?"

"Oh Alex, now you're just being melodramatic."

"That's not an answer, Ali." He leaned over, his face inches from mine. "You've thought about it, haven't you?"

I stared straight into his eyes.

"Answer me, damnit."

I sat there, speechless, trying to think of something clever to say to deflect the tension.

"Son of a bitch. Never mind. That tells me all I need to know." Tears formed in his eyes. He sat back down on the bed, his shoulders slumped. "My God, Ali. I can't take much more."

"Oh, Alex. I'm so sorry." I sat next to him on the edge of the bed, crying. "I don't mean to hurt you; I really don't. I love you. I just can't stand myself right now."

He turned to look at me and took my hands in his. "Ali, I know

142

you're having difficulties. I know what you're doing isn't easy. But I really don't know how much more I can take. If you start getting high again, I can't be sure what I'll do."

"What do you mean? That scares me."

"I'm just saying that I don't know how I'll react. I can't make you any promises."

"What... What does that mean? Are you going to leave me?"

"I'm not sure exactly. I'm just telling you that you do what you have to do, and I'll do what I have to do."

"Honey, please don't say that. I love you so much." I started gasping for breath. "Please tell me you wouldn't leave me."

"I love you, too, sweetheart, but I can't promise you anything. I don't know what I'll do. I only know that I can't take much more. All you ever think about is being high. It's become an obsession, and you haven't even dealt with the effects the sexual abuse has had on your life." He put his arm around me, tears rolling down his cheeks.

All of a sudden I couldn't breathe. I was having another anxiety attack. He rubbed his hand down my back while I gasped for air.

"Calm down, Ali. Come on, breathe slowly."

"Oh my God, I'm so scared!"

"It's okay. Just relax." He handed me a tissue. "Calm and relaxed."

I stood up, trying to catch my breath, but couldn't. I hunched over trying to breathe.

"Lie down on the bed, sweetheart. Come on. Breathe slowly. You're okay. Just relax."

"Alex, please, I love you so much." I lay down with my arms and legs extended. "Please don't leave me. I swear I'll do better."

"It's okay, sweetheart. Calm down. We'll make it through this."

After several minutes, with Alex's help, I began to gain control of my breathing again. "I'll keep going to therapy, okay? I swear. I'll keep trying. Just please help me."

"I'm trying to support you, sweetheart, and be understanding. But you can't just give up."

"I won't. I'll try harder."

"Okay. Scoot over and let me lie beside you."

We lay in the bed, his arm draped over me, my crying stopped.

"I love you, Alex. I'm really sorry for everything. Please just bear with me a little longer. Please."

"I love you too, sweetheart, but something has to change."

"I know. I'll change. I promise."

"Okay. Go to sleep now."

"Thank you," I whispered. "Goodnight."

Chapter 26

The next day I awoke feeling completely exhausted. I lay in bed crying for an hour before I forced myself to get up. While I was in the shower, I gave myself a good talking to and resolved to pull myself together; to stop acting so selfishly.

After showering, I worked a few hours, then listened to classical music while I cleaned house yet again. I took out my frustration and anxiety on the bathtubs, the kitchen sink, and the floors. When I picked up objects to dust I had the urge to fling them across the room, but reminded myself to breathe slowly and kept repeating "calm and relaxed." When Alex walked in from work, the house and I both looked our best and I had dinner in the oven. After dinner we sat at the table and talked for two hours, all remnants of the previous night's outburst seemingly gone. Because he'd gotten so little sleep the night before, he went to bed early. When he said goodnight I felt pretty good. I'd been productive, stayed busy, and made it through another day. I sat up late watching television.

The next morning I woke up tired again. I worked five hours, took a shower, put on my make-up and fixed my hair. I ran a few errands and bought groceries for dinner. After eating I insisted we let the dishes sit, said I'd tend to them later. I joined Alex in the living room and we spent the evening talking about his work, the new project I'd started for work, articles we'd read in the newspaper, movies we wanted to see, and about what we should do during the upcoming week-end. When he went to bed I decided to stay up. Just a little while.

With Alex asleep I was filled with restless energy. I cleaned up the mess I'd made in the kitchen while preparing dinner, then paced the living room floor. I stood staring at books, trying to decide what to read next. Nothing looked interesting. I logged onto the Internet and sent e-mails, apologizing and making excuses to friends for my lack of communication, letting them know I hadn't dropped off the edges of the earth.

After an hour of searching for first editions on the Internet, I made myself a drink. I stood in the kitchen and gulped it down, then made another and wandered into the living room. When I'd finished my fourth drink, I lay down on the couch, curled into a ball, and cried; great, sorrowful, gasping, sobs.

Rage and self-loathing swelled inside me. I sat up on the couch and scratched and dug into my upper arms with my fingernails until my arms bled. I stopped sobbing and ripped ferociously at the skin on my thighs. I sat for a couple of minutes before I took my pocketknife out of my purse and opened the blade. I jabbed the tip of the knife into my forearm a dozen times. I didn't even feel it. I jabbed several more times, harder, until I drew blood. I still hadn't done enough damage. Maybe I could make a quick slice across my arm. Surely I'd feel better then. I sat staring at my arm, trying to decide where to cut.

I almost jumped off the couch when Alex called me from the bedroom. "Ali? Are you okay?"

"Yeah, why?" I quickly folded the blade of my knife and tossed it into my purse.

"I thought I heard you crying." I looked up to see him standing in the bedroom doorway, half asleep. "What are you doing?"

"Nothing," I answered as I crossed my arms. "I'm just feeling a bit anxious. I was crying, but I'm better now. I think I'll take a bubble bath and try to relax. Go back to bed."

"You sure?"

"Yeah, really. Thanks."

"Okay. Goodnight."

"Goodnight. I love you."

I made myself another drink and went into the bathroom. As I slipped into the tub the hot water stung the wounds on my legs. I lay there sipping my drink and staring down at my arms and legs. What had I done? What had come over me? If the damage wasn't staring me full in the face I would've sworn I'd been dreaming. How could I have seriously considered slicing my arm? I must be more whacko than I realized. Alex was right. I was out of control. I really needed to sit down and figure out what I was doing and where I was headed with my life. I stayed in the tub until I finished my drink then stumbled into the kitchen to have just one more. Some time in the early morning I passed out on the couch.

When I awoke the next morning I was surprised to find myself on the couch. I sat up, desperately trying to put together the hours up until I'd passed out. It was no use. I had no idea what had happened the previous night. I stumbled into the bathroom and stepped into the shower, aching to have hot water fall across my body. When I noticed my arms and legs, I was horrified. There were half a dozen places on each of my arms and each of my legs where it looked like the skin had been shredded. The memory slapped me in the face. I'd done it myself. What the hell had happened? I'd have to make sure to wear long-sleeved shirts the next week or so until my arms healed, and be sure to keep them hidden from Alex when I dressed. He'd go berserk if he had any idea what I'd done.

The next few days passed slowly and anxiously. I was still shocked by my previous behavior and every time I caught a glimpse of my arms and legs, I was reminded of the rage I'd felt that night. It scared me to realize I could reach such a point of despair. During my next appointment with Eric I sat anxiously on the couch across from him as we talked. I waited till the session was almost over before I mentioned it.

"I feel like I need to tell you something," I said, "but I don't really want to."

"Okay. What is it?" He leaned toward me, his hands clasped.

"It's really weird. You know, I've never had a relationship with anyone like the one I have with you. It's still hard for me to understand that I can tell you anything and you're not going to get angry or judge me or tell anyone else."

"Well, that's the way it works." He smiled at me. "Really."

"I know."

"What do you want to tell me?"

"Hmmm. It's one of those things where I feel like you need to know because you're my therapist, but I don't want you to know because I'm ashamed."

"Why don't you just go ahead and say it?"

I blurted it out then, telling him about the rage and self-loathing that had overcome me a few nights earlier and what I'd done to myself, how I'd jabbed at my arms with my knife, and how I'd considered slicing my arm.

"Did you go so far as to decide where to cut your arm?"

"Yes. I was going to make a quick slice here, across my forearm."

"What stopped you?"

"I honestly don't know. Maybe because Alex interrupted me. Maybe because I was afraid of the pain. Maybe because I realized what a stupid, whacked out thing it was. I'm really not sure."

"Have you ever done anything like that before?"

"I've scratched my arms and legs before; dug into them with my nails, trying to hurt myself, but I've never considered cutting myself before."

"Have you thought about hurting anyone else?"

"Oh my gosh, no. I couldn't ever hurt anyone." I started crying softly. "I only hate myself."

"What were you thinking at the time?"

"That I can't get the fucking pictures out of my head. That I can't get Jack's and Scott's voices out of my brain. That I can't get rid of the anger now that I don't have drugs or alcohol to numb the pain. That I need to do something to release the rage. And a knife seemed a good way."

"Does Alex know about this?"

"Oh, God, no."

"What do you think he'd say?"

"He'd go berserk!"

"So, you're doing this after Alex goes to bed. When you're alone."

"Yes." I didn't look at Eric, just sat playing with the fringe on the afghan laying across the couch.

"You always act like you're in control when others are around. Always have your game face on, don't you?"

"Yep."

"Then when you're alone, you release the anger. When no one's looking."

"Yeah, I guess."

I glanced up at him. He sat there a minute, not speaking, just watching me.

"If you could draw the way you felt, what would the drawing look like?"

"I don't know. It'd be black."

"Ali, next time this rage builds inside you I want you to try to draw it or write about it. Then let's take a look at that and find some way for you to put words to the feelings. You've got to find another way to express your feelings – without alcohol or drugs or slicing your arm. Will you do that?"

"Sure, I guess."

"You understand you've got to turn the anger away from yourself, direct it outward?"

"Yes."

"When do you see Dr. McCain again?"

"Early next week. I'm a bit anxious about that. You think he's going to make me go back to rehab?"

"I can't say. I'd start, though, by not being drunk or stoned when you arrived."

"I know. I won't."

"Okay. See you next week?"

"Sure."

"If you need to, you can call me before then."

"Yeah, I know. Thanks."

Chapter 27

When I left Eric's office I was relieved I'd told him about my impulse to cut my arm. He'd done well; fallen back on that good old therapist training of not showing any emotion or shock. I decided I was most likely one of his saner clients, though, and he probably wished I'd just leave him the hell alone; stop whining, stop feeling sorry for myself, and stop bothering him with my petty inconsequential problems. I know I was certainly sick of it.

I drove to the nearest bookstore. A couple of hours later I returned home, still feeling anxious, but more relaxed than I'd been earlier. I spent the next few days working, trying new recipes for supper, and generally trying to keep busy. I talked on the phone to friends and assured them I was doing great; everything was wonderful. I did my best to be pleasant around Alex and I stayed clean and sober. At night I paced the living room floor, surfed the Web, updated my book database, and wrote in my journal. Once again I felt like screaming.

I was concerned about my upcoming meeting with Dr. McCain. It would be my first visit with him since he'd discontinued our sessions. I wasn't quite sure what to expect. And I was concerned Eric may have told him about my episode with the knife.

As I sat in the waiting room I listened to Christian rock music on my headphones. Dr. McCain finally came for me.

"So, Ali, how are you?" he asked as soon as we were settled.

I knew it wasn't polite chitchat this time.

"Doing okay," I answered. "I haven't smoked for twenty-six days!" I wanted to impress him right off, before he had a chance to chastise me about anything, in case Eric had gotten to him before I had.

"What about alcohol? How long has it been since you had a drink?"

"Uh, five days."

He looked at me, hand and pen suspended above his notepad. "Why not longer?"

"But it's been twenty-six days since I smoked or took a pill," I repeated, somewhat less enthusiastically.

"I know. And that's great. I don't want to diminish that accomplishment. But why has it only been five days since you drank?"

"I don't know. I just got fed up the other day, said screw it and made myself a drink." I slumped on the couch.

"Did you get drunk?"

"Yes," I said, feeling more and more like I was visiting my parole officer and not my psychiatrist.

"When was the last time you experienced a blackout?"

"The last time I drank," I answered, self-conscious and ashamed.

"What about AA, NA, or MA?" He wrote in my chart as he talked. "Are you attending meetings?"

"No."

"Why not?"

"I really don't like them."

"I understand. And I agree they can be tedious, but how are you going to stay clean and sober without support from other addicts?"

I wanted to jump off the couch, then, and scream at him that I wasn't an addict. Couldn't anybody get that through their thick skull? I only drank a little, smoked some dope, and took a few pills. Addicts used crack and heroin and didn't bathe or work or do anything else. They lived in hovels, spending their time looking for ways to pay for their next fix. They were really sick people in need of serious help and they had my full sympathy. I, on the other hand, only needed the people around me to stop being so damn prudish.

"I can do it by myself," I answered. "I don't want to attend meetings."

"I'll let it go for now. But I want you to consider going to some meetings. I'd feel much better then. What has Eric said about testing?"

"That he'd take my word that I wasn't doing drugs and that he'd only request a UDS if my behavior caused him to become suspicious."

"Okay. I'll go along with that."

I breathed a sigh of relief. No more rehab.

"Do you have anything else you want to discuss?"

"No," I blurted. "Everything's fine."

"Okay, then." He handed me a prescription. "I want you to begin taking the Trazadone at night again. Let's see you back here in three weeks."

I couldn't believe it. I'd made it! I was anxious to get home and celebrate, but didn't know how to do that without smoking or drinking.

My excitement didn't last very long. The next day I had another anxiety attack, this time while sitting at my computer working. I'd been so concerned about getting out of Dr. McCain's office without any mention of the knife, that I'd forgotten to mention the anxiety attacks to him. That night I made a point to take my medicine early and go to bed at the same time as Alex. No more pacing the floors for me. I was asleep within the hour.

I'd made it through another day, but the anxiety attack scared me and I didn't relish the prospect of facing another day without chemical help. After I showered the next morning I called my dealer. Maybe one joint or a few pills was all I needed until this anxiety thing passed. Then I'd quit. I let the phone ring fifteen times, but he didn't answer. Although it went against all the rules, I took a chance and called him at work. He was out of town on a business trip and wouldn't return for four days. Damn.

I spent another day working, cleaning house, and cooking. I tried to read, but every time I picked up a book the words stayed on the page instead of jumping into my imagination. I hadn't read a whole book in months. I was clean and sober, but life was as dull as a rock. Might as well roll over and play dead. What was the fucking point? How could people stand to live like this?

Once again I joined Alex when he went to bed. Although I'd taken my medicine, two hours later I was still wide awake. I couldn't stand it any longer. I got out of bed and walked the floors. A feeling of numbness crept over my whole body and I couldn't shake it. I really needed to get high, but I didn't have anything and I didn't want to disappoint Alex by drinking. Besides, I'd either have to lie or report my use to Dr. McCain and Eric, my keepers. What was I going to do? I sat on the edge of the couch crying softly.

Then it came to me. I took the pocketknife out of my purse and opened the blade. I sat for a minute, staring at the knife, then at my arm. Where should I cut? My forearm was out of the question I realized. I needed a place that wasn't so conspicuous. It would look a bit weird if I walked around outside wearing a long-sleeved shirt in 98 degree heat. Finally, I rolled up the sleeve of the t-shirt I was wearing and with my right hand made a slash on my upper left arm. It soothed me immediately. I made another cut and watched the blood ooze from the wounds. I walked to the kitchen, jerked a paper towel off the rack and applied it to my arm. When the bleeding was somewhat under control, I slashed my arm again, enjoying the sharpness of the pain as it dulled my anxiety. When I'd made half a dozen cuts, I stopped. I felt immensely calm. I attended to the bleeding and went to bed.

While dressing the next morning I noticed the cuts on my arms. I'd forgotten about them, but I wasn't disgusted upon seeing them. I felt strangely indifferent. Throughout the day when the sleeve of my shirt brushed my arm and caused me a moment's discomfort, I enjoyed it. It was like a shot of adrenaline.

As I was changing clothes that night, Alex walked into the bedroom. I experienced a flash of panic and hurriedly turned my body to shield my arm from his view. I grabbed a t-shirt and pulled it over my head. Close call. That was all I needed now – Alex freaking out on me. I'd have to be more careful in the future. Maybe cuts on my legs would be easier to hide. I'd better prepare a couple of stories to account for the cuts in case he did notice.

Chapter 28

As the week passed I continued to feel anxious and depressed, wondering what in hell the big deal was about life. Why all the hoopla? When Alex and I went to the movies I was unable to conjure up any feelings for the characters. When a hero or heroine died and people in the audience cried, I thought, what's the big fuss? It's just death. Why do people get so worked up about it? You live and then you die. The end.

I fantasized about drugs and alcohol, as well as cutting myself. I would definitely try my leg next time.

Two days before my appointment with Eric I considered calling and canceling. Why bother to continue? I didn't see that it was doing me any good. Actually, in my humble opinion, it all sucked. Yeah, I was clean and sober – big fucking deal. I was also miserable, edgy, tense, and anxious; on the verge of crying and throwing up every second of the day. Everyone could go to hell in a hand basket as far as I was concerned. I just wanted to take the edge off and I didn't care what the consequences were.

I was the good girl, though, and followed through with my appointment. By the time I walked into Eric's office, I'd pretty much reached the limits of my patience. I came out swinging.

When he asked how I was feeling I jumped up from the couch and paced around his office.

"Horrible," I answered.

"I'm glad to hear that."

"What? That I'm feeling horrible?"

"Yes. You come in here week after week and tell me you're down a little bit or everything's fine. It's nice to hear you're finally beginning to realize that you're not okay. Admit that you feel horrible sometimes."

"Gee, thanks." I sat down in a chair on the other side of the room.

"So what's going on?"

"I can't stand this. I hate living without chemicals. It's awful!" I stood up and paced again.

"It gets better," he answered.

155

"Yeah, well, that's what people keep telling me. I'm not so sure I believe them." I sat back down. "Damnit. I really hate this."

"What have you been doing?"

"You mean besides trying to retain my sanity?"

"Yes."

"Nothing. Not a damn thing. All the usual. You know, cooking, cleaning, working. All that crap. Bitching, whining, griping."

"Sounds like you're a real joy to be around."

"Oh, yeah, don't you know." I stood up again. "I don't know what to tell you. I just can't get rid of these feelings. I don't know what to do. Sorry. I feel like I'm wasting our session."

"That's okay." He waited till I settled on the couch again. "Ali, you need to talk about the abuse and your feelings. Not just wrap the anger around you."

"Oh, God. I know. I just don't know how." I leaned over, rested my head in my hands and stared at the floor. "I feel like I should be past all that. Why do I obsess about it? Why don't I just move on with my life?"

"It doesn't work like that. The sub-conscious doesn't tell time. It might as well have happened yesterday. And when you're victimized, you do things just to survive. You have to remember that you were a child and the people entrusted to take care of you abused you instead. They lied to you and manipulated you and that's affected your whole life."

"I understand what you're saying, but I feel like I'm using that as an excuse and that I should just be strong and move on. You know, 'Pull yourself together, Ali. Be tough.'" I looked up at him, tears sliding down my cheeks. "God, you must be sick of me saying that over and over. I know I am."

He chuckled. "That's okay. I realize it's hard to grasp. Your whole life's been about you being tough and holding everything in, but that's why you're here today. You really do have to deal with it. You can pretend to be tough, but in the end you're right back where you were twenty years ago; angry, hurt, and confused."

I wiped the tears away with the back of my hand and tried to smile.

"It's okay to cry, Ali." He sat there a moment, not speaking. "It

156

wasn't your fault. You can't continue to blame yourself."

"I should have stopped it."

"How could you have done that? You were just a child."

"I could have done something, said something."

"You survived. That's what's important. You did what you had to do to survive."

I looked away from him, not answering.

"And you used drugs and alcohol to cope," he continued. "But now you have to learn different coping techniques."

"Yeah, I know. I just don't know how."

"That's what I'm here for. To teach you. You can do this, you know."

"I know."

"Do you think anybody understands what you're going through right now?"

"No. I know Alex tries and so does Matt and our other friends. But they don't have a clue. I'm sure they think it's just a matter of me quitting. They can't understand the obsession and compulsion. People talk about how hard it is to stop smoking cigarettes and it is, I know, because I did it. But this is a million times worse. Knowing that a drink or a few hits off a joint or a couple of pills would take the edge off. Knowing it's out there for you, but you're not supposed to touch it."

"You think you could try to explain your emotions to Alex?"

"No. I mean I've tried, but I know people get impatient and tired of hearing about it. No one could possibly understand the shame and anger and rage and guilt unless they'd been through it. And I've talked up a blue streak about the abuse, trying to find some way to understand it. But in the end, no matter what I say or how many times I say it, Alex can't fix it or make it go away. So," I laughed, "I have to pay you to listen to me."

"Oh well." He grinned. "It's not too terrible. What else is going on with you? Has Alex been traveling much?"

"No. He's been home a lot lately."

"That's good."

"Yeah, normally. But right now I don't care. I rather like being alone."

"Why?"

"So I can do whatever I want." I smoothed the fringe on the afghan. "Not worry about what anybody thinks."

"You're always concerned with what others think, aren't you? You've become a master at hiding your true feelings. What do you do when you're alone that you can't do when you're with others?"

"Get high. Get drunk. Listen to loud music." Cut myself, I thought.

"What else?"

"I don't know. Nothing."

"What about your knife? Have you had the urge to jab yourself with a knife again?"

I looked at him out of the corner of my eye, not answering. I couldn't think what to say.

"Have you done it again?"

"No, not really."

"What does 'not really' mean? What exactly have you done?"

I curled up inside, tried to push myself as far back on the couch as possible.

"Ali?"

I stared at him, unsure what to say. "I cut my arm."

"Where?"

"Here." I slapped at my upper arm.

"Oh, up high, so it wouldn't be noticeable."

"Yeah."

"How much did you cut?

"I don't know. Half a dozen slashes."

"How deep did you cut?"

"Not too bad."

"Superficial cuts?"

"Yes."

"Was there any bleeding?"

"Yes, but not much."

"You know cutting isn't the answer, Ali."

"Yeah, I know. But I..."

"You what?"

"Nothing."

158

"You slipped, didn't you? What were you going to say?"

I glanced at him, wondering if I was ever going to learn to keep my mouth shut.

"Ali, what were you going to say?"

"I, uh... I like it."

"You know that's not good. It's not going to solve any of your problems."

"I know, but I don't know what else to do. You and Dr. McCain took away my drugs and alcohol. Are you going to take this away from me, too?"

"No. We can't take it away. You're going to have to do it."

"But I don't want to."

"Hopefully that will change."

I didn't bother to respond.

"I promise you, Ali, that things are going to get better as long as you stay with the program; clean and sober. And continue to meet with Dr. McCain and me. I know it goes against everything you've learned about men, but you have to trust us. Will you do that?"

"Sure, I guess."

"Okay, then. See you next week."

Chapter 29

All the way home I fantasized about cutting my leg. I'd have to do it up high so it wouldn't be noticeable when I was wearing shorts. And I should probably clean the knife blade this time.

I stopped at the grocery store to pick up some things for supper. I certainly didn't want Alex to detect the awful mood I was in and start asking too many questions. When he arrived home from work I was in the kitchen cooking and trying to talk myself into cheering up. I had a smile on my face when he walked in.

"Hi darling. How are you?" I gave him a kiss.

"Feeling good. How about you?"

"I'm great," I lied. "You want a cocktail?"

"Sure. Thanks."

After he changed clothes we sat in the living room talking as we sipped our drinks; rum and Coke for him, iced tea for me.

"So, tell me about your day," I said.

"Oh, not much to tell. Saw a few clients, had a couple of cancellations. Had one new client. A man suffering from depression. I'd rather hear more about your day, though. You saw Eric, didn't you?"

"Uh-huh."

"How'd that go? You want to talk about it?"

"It was pretty much the same old thing. Him trying to convince me to put the blame where it belongs; stop blaming myself. I don't know. It's really hard. I feel all mixed up inside. I can't explain it."

He nodded.

"It's weird. It's like when you're trying to do a lot of things at once and you feel like your brain's going to explode, trying to retain and keep track of so many things, you know? Well that's how my insides feel. Like my heart's going to explode from all the conflicting emotions bouncing around inside me. I don't know how to maintain any degree of calm."

"I'm sorry you're going through this, sweetheart. But it really will get better. I guess it's kind of like basic training in the Army. It sucks while you're going through it, but you end up a stronger person as a result of having gone through it."

"I know you're right." I smiled at him. "It's just that sometimes I wish I wouldn't have enlisted."

"I know, sweetheart. I'm really proud of you for staying with it."

If he knew I was cutting myself he wouldn't be so proud. I really had to make sure he didn't find out. At least not until way down the road when I was well. Then it wouldn't matter what kind of madness I'd gone through to get there.

"Ali?"

"Huh, what?"

"I asked when your next appointment is with Dr. McCain."

"Oh, sorry. In a couple of weeks. I think he wants to keep a close watch on me for awhile. It's so weird. I feel like I'm reporting to a confessor, listing my sins. But I know it's my own fault. He and Eric did give me plenty of chances. I really hate it, though. I don't want to be a so-called addict. I want to get high. Oh crap. That doesn't make any sense, does it? If I didn't have a chemical dependency problem, then I wouldn't care, would I?"

Alex didn't answer. He realized they were rhetorical questions and let me chatter on.

"Oh, Alex. I feel so mixed up. I feel like I don't know what to do. My feelings change from one minute to the next, then back again." I started crying. "What am I going to do?"

"I think just what you've been doing. Stay away from the drugs and alcohol and continue therapy. You've just got to hang tough."

"God, I'm sick of hearing that. I'm sorry. I didn't mean that. Except that's just what Eric told me today. It's going to get better, hang in there, blah, blah, blah." The tears came harder now and I longed for a drink. "I just wish the bastards never would've touched me."

"I'm so sorry, Ali. I wish I could make it all go away; that you could be happy."

"I know. Thanks. I'm sorry I keep getting weird on you."

I went to the bathroom to get a tissue, then into the kitchen to make him a fresh drink and top off my iced tea. My crying had finally stopped by the time I returned to the living room.

"Did I tell you I went to see Dr. Chambers, my dentist, yesterday afternoon? Remember, I had those two teeth that were hurting?" I handed him his drink and took a seat on the couch.

"Thanks. Oh, that's right. What did he say?"

"Turns out I've got abscesses under each of them. Isn't that exciting? Because I have root canals and there are crowns on both teeth, I have to go to a specialist so he can drill into the crowns to do root canals. At least that's the way I understand it. Then back to my dentist to finish it up. Wonder how much that's going to cost?"

"I keep telling you not to worry so much about money, Ali. When are you going?"

"That's another thing. I couldn't get an appointment with the specialist for three weeks." I studied the ice in my glass.

"Did he give you anything in the meantime?"

"What do you mean?"

"You know, antibiotics?"

"Oh, yeah."

"Did he suggest anything for the pain?"

I continued to stare at the ice.

"Sweetheart, did he say anything?"

"Yeah. He gave me a prescription."

"Oh. What kind of prescription exactly?"

"Pain pills."

He paused with his glass halfway to his mouth. "What kind of pain pills?"

"Vicodin."

He set his drink on the end table. "I don't guess you mentioned that you're an addict and shouldn't have pain medication except as a last resort?"

"No, I didn't mention that."

"Have you taken any?"

"Yeah, I took one. But only..."

"Oh, Ali. Why..."

"Wait. I only took one to see what kind of reaction I'd have. I think Vicodin's what they give to people who are allergic to codeine, but not everyone tolerates it well. So you see, I just took it as kind of a test."

"Yeah, sure, I see."

"Really, I swear."

"And what are you going to do with the pills that are left?"

"Well, I planned on keeping them. Just in case my mouth starts hurting real bad."

He guzzled the remainder of his drink. "Great plan, Ali."

"Besides, I'm not convinced I'm an addict, remember? I hate that term. It just doesn't apply to me. It's not like I'm doing drugs or drinking every day."

"It's not all the time only because you're forcing yourself to abstain. A casual user of alcohol or drugs doesn't have to force themselves to abstain. And, as you well know, addiction is a state of mind, a thought process. Quantity and frequency aren't litmus tests for addiction. I'm sure Eric's told you the simple fact that if you plan your usage and strategize about when and where is a sign of dependency. Damnit, Ali, you were sitting around here barely able to carry on a conversation with me at night, just wishing I'd go to bed so you could get drunk and stoned."

"But I..."

"Do you disagree?"

"Well, no. But..."

"There are no buts, Ali. Why don't you simply admit it? Why are you fighting it so?"

"I don't know. I just feel like once I allow myself to be labeled an alcoholic or an addict, then there's no turning back. It's there forever."

"It's there forever whether you label it or not, sweetheart. Some people are diabetic, some have asthma, and some suffer from chemical dependency. Ignoring it won't make it go away."

I started crying then, a great torrent of tears falling down my cheeks. "Oh God, Alex. I'm so scared. I feel like I'm slipping away. I don't know what to do. Please help me."

He stood up and walked over to where I was sitting. "Come here, sweetheart."

When I stood up he wrapped his arms around me. "I love you, Ali. It's going to be alright. Really, it is." He kissed the top of my head. "Just hold on, sweetheart. You can do this."

I cried on his shoulder, gasping and gulping, as I tried to breathe.

He ran his fingers through my hair and rubbed my back. "Ssh. It's okay, hon."

I looked up at him. "I'm sorry to be such a pain." I tried to smile.

He kissed me on the cheek, then on the mouth. When I responded, he started kissing my neck as he ran both hands down my back. He took my hand and led me into the bedroom.

We made love, softly and tenderly. It was the first time in months that I was able to enjoy it; an outpouring of love and affection instead of a feeling of being used and exploited. For the first time in a long time I didn't have to constantly remind myself that it was okay, that it was Alex, a man who truly loved me. For the life of me, though, I couldn't understand why. I fell asleep in his arms as he stroked my hair and face.

Chapter 30

My next appointment with Eric was uneventful. Just more rehashing of the same old things; blame, guilt, shame, rage, and on and on. When the session ended without him asking about my cutting, I felt I'd won a small victory. He and Dr. McCain may be able to request a UDS from me at any time, but they certainly couldn't make me strip down so they could check for slashes on my body. I was back in control.

Over the next couple of weeks, my sessions with Eric became more intense. We talked about the sexual abuse and I spent the time either ranting and raving about my hatred for men or sitting on the couch, crying, unable to express my shame and anger, while Eric reiterated that it wasn't my fault and that I had to learn new ways of coping with my feelings.

I continued to cut my arms and legs and was a mess of healing wounds as well as fresh ones. Eric questioned me about it quite often, but he knew there wasn't much point in discussing it. I think he really just wanted to let me know that he was aware of it. In the meantime he tried to help me learn other ways to express my feelings. When Alex was home I had to be careful to change clothes when he wasn't in the same room. Often I went into the bathroom before undressing, and at night I made sure the lights were out before I slipped into bed. I had a horrible fear that he was going to either see the cuts or feel the raised scars on my arms and legs.

In the evenings we spent time talking, watching television, playing Scrabble, or going out with friends. During the day I worked, cleaned, cooked, and had little chats with myself, reminders to focus on something besides me. I'd always said that people who spent time worrying about themselves obviously had too much time on their hands. Here I was now, one of those people. I didn't have too much time on my hands, but was too self-absorbed I decided, and needed to stop obsessing about the past.

Two days before my next appointment with Dr. McCain I spent the whole morning in a bookstore looking for first editions. I'd given up trying to read anything for awhile. I simply wasn't able to concentrate. For that matter I was hardly eating. Nothing, it seemed, could hold my interest except my own issues. I really disliked the person I had become and kept telling myself to grow up and to get a life.

Driving home from the bookstore I listened to *Counting Crows* and Fiona Apple in the car while my mood went from bad to horrible. I considered calling my dealer from my cell phone and running by his place for a quick pick-me-up, but common sense won over and I drove straight home. Five minutes from the house I thought to hell with everyone and decided to get good and drunk.

I walked in the door, set my down purse, threw the mail on the coffee table, and lay on my back on the couch, letting my feet dangle over the end. I really needed to get a grip on my state of mind. I did some deep breathing and self relaxation and eventually fell asleep. The next thing I knew Alex was walking in from work. I'd made it; I'd stayed sober.

We had a nice dinner and talked about our day before he left to shoot pool. He hadn't been gone thirty minutes when I made myself a drink. I gulped it down and immediately made another. I decided I could rot in self-pity if I wanted. After all, it was my damn life, not anyone else's. Why was I allowing so many other people so much control?

When I was on my third drink I pulled the pocketknife out of my purse. I opened the blade and stared at it for a full minute. I looked forward to the cutting. I rolled up my shorts, gently ran the tip of the blade across my upper thigh, teasingly, barely scratching the skin. I stared at the blade once more before actually cutting, this time slicing hard and fast; a horizontal cut. The blood dripped out. I ripped a paper towel from the holder and placed it against my leg, concerned the blood would fall onto my freshly mopped kitchen floor. I waited a few seconds, then made a second cut. There were six slashes on my leg before I was able to quit.

Once again I sat anxiously waiting for Dr. McCain to call me in for our session. After the usual formalities he got right to the inquisition.

"So, how long have you been clean?"

"Forty-one days," I answered, thinking, "Forgive me, Dr., it's been six weeks since my last confession."

"Good for you, that's great." He looked down at my chart as he made notes.

"How long since your last drink?"

"Two days." I said it boldly. Maybe they were right; a good offense was the best defense.

His head jerked up. "Two days?"

"Yes," I answered, the boldness deflated like a punctured balloon.

"What happened?"

"I don't know. I just couldn't stand it anymore and I made myself a drink."

"Did you get drunk?"

"Yes."

He set the pen down on top of my chart and looked up at me. Uh-oh, not a good sign.

"Eric tells me you've been cutting," he said.

Oh, hell. I wasn't ready for that. I was waiting for the drug abuse and AA lecture. I sat there stunned. What an idiot. How could I have been so naïve? Of course he and Eric must talk. I'd been lulled into a false sense of security since Dr. McCain hadn't mentioned the cutting during our last session. Damn. What should I say?

"Ali?"

Act stupid. "Oh, I'm sorry. What did you say?"

"Is it true? That you've been cutting?"

"Well, um, yeah, a little."

"Tell me about that."

"What do you mean?"

"How many times have you cut yourself?" he asked.

"I don't know. A few."

"You mean a few cuts or a few different occasions?"

"A few different occasions."

"I see." He bent his head and began scribbling in my chart again.

Great, just what I needed. A permanent record of my madness. Maybe he wasn't writing about me. Maybe therapists and shrinks the world over actually sat there doodling, looking at the clock, wishing the hell they'd chosen a different profession. Maybe a horse trainer or jockey; something as far away from people as they could possibly get; away from whining, self-destructive, self-absorbed brats.

He looked back up at me. "What happens before you cut? How are you feeling?"

"I don't know. Angry and anxious, I guess, and indifferent. I know that doesn't make sense, but I don't seem to care about anything; writing, food, books, Alex. I just feel like I don't give a rat's ass about what happens to me or to anyone for that matter. I feel like I'm just going through the motions. But at the same time I feel like I'm going to scream if I don't do something. I don't know how else to explain it. So I cut and I feel better."

"Have you been thinking about suicide?"

"No, just destruction."

"Do you feel hopeless?"

"No, not really. I mean I kind of do, but not deep down."

"I'd like to double your Zyprexa, see how that works for you. It should help even out your mood swings some more as well as diminish your urge to cut. But, I'm telling you this, Ali, you have to give up the alcohol and drugs. Don't play me for a fool. It only makes me angry."

"Oh, I wouldn't do that," I almost shouted. "Really."

"Okay then. Let's see how this new dosage works."

"Should I continue taking the Prozac?"

"Yes. That's it, then. I want to see you back in three weeks, though."

Damn. That was close. Better watch my step.

Chapter 31

The next several weeks passed slowly and miserably. I was seeing Eric on a weekly basis, discussing the sexual abuse and learning to direct my anger outward. The new dosage of the Zyprexa had lessened the extremity of my mood swings and had helped me to stop cutting. I still had the urge, but was able to resist and my wounds finally healed. It was the same with the alcohol and drugs. Every day I considered getting high and drinking, but pushed myself through the day, sometimes in fifteen minute increments. I still hadn't attended any Alcoholics Anonymous or Narcotics Anonymous meetings, but Dr. McCain hadn't been so insistent since I'd been able to stay clean and sober on my own. He said he'd feel more comfortable if I had a support system in place, but he didn't press the issue.

My therapy with Eric was progressing, but it was painfully slow. I wanted to simply wake up one morning and be well; free of the shame and guilt I'd felt for years, and free of the compulsion to drink and get high. It wasn't that easy, though, and I fought daily to maintain some degree of balance.

Alex and I were getting along well. He was extremely pleased with the clean and sober me. However, I still wore my game face. I hadn't yet grasped the technique of letting others see me with my guard down. I was either putting up a front, being bright and cheerful, or sitting in my office with the door closed, needing to be alone with my anxiety and agitation and tears.

Finally, after more than three horribly long months of clean and sober living, I reached my breaking point. I'm not really sure what happened. One morning I got out of bed, ate breakfast, worked three hours, then sat at my desk sobbing. Fuck it, I thought, and called my dealer. After assuring him I hadn't fallen off the planet during my conspicuous absence, I asked if he had any Ecstasy, Liquid X, coke, speed, anything. No more Mickey Mouse crap. I wanted real drugs. He said he had half an ounce of pot, but could have more for me in the next day or so. As far as the other stuff, he was out of everything except Percodan. Damn. We arranged a time and place to meet.

Two hours later I was home smoking a joint, lying on the floor listening to music, drinking a vodka and 7, and waiting for the Percodan to kick in. I was on top of the world. Everything was great for the first time in months.

When Alex arrived home he was stunned. I didn't know what to say to him. I had no reason or excuse for my behavior. There obviously wasn't anything I could do to make it better. The damage was done. I remembered the many times Daddy had sworn he'd stopped drinking for good, only to go on a two week binge a few days later. And I remembered my feelings of betrayal, disappointment, sadness, and anger. Now I'd done the same thing to Alex.

Alex and I hardly spoke the whole evening. He fixed himself something to eat and watched television as I continued to lie on the floor, listening to music through the headphones. He gave me a quick kiss before going to bed early. I lay on the floor crying, wondering what the hell I had done. What was wrong with me? Why had I screwed things up again? Anger washed over me. I grabbed my knife from my purse. I didn't bother to clean the blade. I stumbled to the laundry room to get a towel from the rag pile, then sat on the floor with the towel under my leg. With deep, savage thrusts I made several cut across my left leg. I watched with morbid satisfaction as the blood flowed.

I guzzled down the remainder of my drink, wiped the blade on the towel, and sliced into my other leg. Afterwards I didn't hesitate. I immediately cut into my upper left arm on top of the wounds that had finally healed in the past few months. When I finished that arm I switched the blade to my left hand and began cutting my right arm. The self-loathing and anger raged inside me. I sat a moment, crying great sorrowful sobs. I hesitated only a moment before I made a diagonal slice across each of my breasts. My anger spent, I smoked a joint while I lay on the towel and wept.

At 2:00 in the morning I dialed Eric's voice mail and pressed one to leave him a message.

"Hi Eric, it's me," I muttered, "Ali Connery. I need help. Please call me tomorrow if you can."

I hung up, crawled to the couch to retrieve the afghan, laid it over me to hide the damage I'd done, then passed out on the living room floor.

I was awakened by the ringing of the telephone. I glanced at the clock on the VCR, 9:00 a.m. What day was it? Tuesday, Wednesday? Guess Alex had already left for work. Don't remember him telling me goodbye.

Why was I on the floor? Had I slept there? Had Alex and I fought? When I fumbled for the ringing phone, the afghan fell away from me. I saw the blood then and remembered the cutting.

"Hello?" I muttered, my mouth dry and foul.

"Hi Ali, it's Eric."

"Oh, hi."

"How are you? You didn't sound too good when you called."

"I called you?"

"Yes. You left a message at 2:00 this morning asking me to call you today. You don't remember?"

"Uh, yeah, I guess."

"What's going on?"

"Oh, God. I think I've really screwed up this time."

"What happened?"

I started crying. "I'm not sure. I was drunk and high last night when Alex got home from work. I think he might be mad at me," I sobbed. "And I cut myself again." I looked down at the blood soaked towel I'd slept on and the crisscross of slashes on my body.

"Are you okay? Do you need to go to the doctor?"

"Yes. I mean no, I don't need to see a doctor; yes, I'm okay."

"Can you make it in to see me this morning? Let's say in about two hours?"

"Yeah, sure, I guess."

"Good. I'll look for you at 11:00."

I forced myself to empty the ashtray, put the bottle of Vodka away and put my empty glass in the dishwasher. When I picked the towel up off the floor I saw that the blood had soaked through to the carpet. Damn. I'd really made a mess. Alex would be furious. I grabbed the bottle of carpet cleaner and a damp rag to see if I could get the blood out. I tamped and blotted for the better part of five minutes until I'd succeeded in cleaning up the bulk of it. I took a look at the afghan. There were spots of blood on it as well. Oh, great. It had been a wedding present. I threw it in the washer with the towels. Couldn't do much more damage to it I figured.

The smell of pot and vodka clung to me. Visions leaped into my brain of alcohol actually seeping from my pores while a cloud of Marijuana smoke followed me wherever I walked, like Linus in the Peanuts comic strip. I thought it extremely possible I may be on the next cover of *The Inquirer*.

I took an Imitrex for my migraine and immediately vomited. I sipped some water then swirled Scope in my mouth. I vomited again. I lay on the bathroom floor holding a wet washcloth against my forehead. When I felt well enough, I forced myself to stand up to brush my teeth. I vomited again, regurgitating vodka and water.

Finally I stumbled into the shower. The hot water stung my cuts as I stood there trying to pull myself together. I rested my arms and head against the towel bar, letting the water flow down my shoulders and back. I stood like that for ten minutes, weeping.

"So, you want to tell me what happened?" Eric asked the moment I entered his office.

"I'm not sure. I was doing really well, you know. It'd been about three months since I'd gotten high or drank. But last night something just went off inside me and I couldn't stand it another minute. I felt like I was going to explode if I didn't do something, so I lit a joint, took a couple of Percodan, and made myself a drink." I sat on the couch rubbing my temples, wondering when the Imitrex I'd finally been able to keep down would kick in.

"Did you get drunk?"

"Yeah. I pretty much smoked and drank until I passed out on the floor."

"On the phone you mentioned you've been cutting again."

"Yes, but I don't really remember a whole lot. Mostly I remember the anger and rage inside me and how I couldn't get rid of it. If Alex hadn't been in the next room, I probably would've screamed. I ended up cutting myself instead." I leaned over, holding my head in my hands. "I've really screwed up this time."

"How so?"

"Well. Oh, God, I really don't want to say."

174

"What is it, Ali? Just say it."

"Well, this time I also cut my breasts."

"And you don't remember doing that?"

"No. And when I got out of the shower this morning there was a message from my dealer on our voice mail. He said for me to call him back and when I did he told me he'd been able to score the crack and Ecstasy I'd called him about; that I could meet him sometime today to pick everything up." I glanced up at Eric.

"I'm assuming you don't remember making that call either?"

"No, I don't. Of course I remember talking to him yesterday afternoon and going to buy the pot and the pills. I mean, I was sober then. I guess I must've called him again later in the evening to ask about the other stuff. I just don't know." Tears slipped from my eyes. "Oh, God."

"Ali, after I spoke with you this morning I had a quick meeting with Dr. McCain." He looked at his watch. "He has an opening in fifteen minutes and would like to talk to you. Will you do that?

"Oh, hell. I guess so, yeah."

I went into the ladies room to freshen up before seeing Dr. McCain. When I'd arrived at Eric's office I wasn't exactly looking my best. Evidently getting drunk and high, then sleeping on the floor wasn't a beauty tip I'd be reading any time soon in *Cosmopolitan*.

And after crying in Eric's office, I was in no condition to be seen in public. One look in the mirror was enough to convince me I could cause lifelong trauma to vulnerable children. I repaired the damage as best I could without actually resorting to cosmetic surgery, then sat in my violet chair in the waiting room.

After several minutes of wringing my hands and tapping my foot, Dr. McCain called for me. Damn, did I dread this little chat.

"Hello Ali. Have a seat." He waved me toward the couch.

I smiled big. "Hi, how are you?" I asked, all sunshine and cheer.

"I'm fine, thanks." No smile from him. Guess he saw straight through my little ruse. "Obviously you know that Eric and I have spoken."

"Yes."

"How long had you been clean and sober? Three months?"

"Yes."

"I'm sorry to have to say this, Ali, but I'm recommending you go to rehab."

"No, please! Not more IOP. I don't think I could bear it."

"I'm not talking about IOP. I'm talking about the twenty-eight day program."

"What? Are you serious?"

"I'm afraid so. I just don't see you dealing with this by yourself."

I sat there in disbelief, bent over, resting my head in my hands, rocking back and forth.

"Eric and I also agree that you should start attending group therapy for sexual abuse victims. There's a meeting once a week at A Woman's Place."

I started crying then, undoing the fine work I'd so painstakingly completed in the ladies room a short while earlier. I stole a glance at him before resuming my rocking.

"Would I still see you and Eric?"

"Of course. I'd see you over there. And you'd continue your sessions with Eric when you completed rehab; then continue coming to my office as well."

"Oh God. Do I really have to?"

"No, you don't have to." My heart skipped a beat. "But I'll remind you that I can't continue to see you or prescribe medication in light of your recent behavior."

"But it was only one slip!"

"You know that's not true. You've been going back and forth for months and I'm just not going to allow it anymore. You've got to get help, Ali. You know that."

"I know," I muttered.

"I'm concerned about the cutting, as well."

"Oh, yeah. I forgot."

"You realize that cutting is a way of dealing with emotional discomfort and it's imperative that you develop other coping skills."

"Yeah, I know, Eric's told me."

"And it's also dangerous."

"I don't cut too deep, though," I protested.

"No, not now. But cutting is progressive. Besides, if you're cutting when you're drunk or stoned you could easily go too far."

176

I didn't respond. After last night's debacle I didn't feel I had the right to disagree or argue. I was fresh out of excuses and justifications. It was plainly evident I'd lost the war.

"So you'll go?"

"Oh God. I guess so. I don't know what else to do." Tears fell to my lap.

He gave me instructions for checking in at Whispering Pines. I left his office and made my way to the waiting room. I didn't bother to wipe away the tears that rolled down my cheeks. I didn't care who looked at me or what they might think.

I drove straight home, shocked and afraid of what was to come. What would Alex say? What would I do in rehab for twenty-eight days? What about my work? What about the bills? What about the cost? What about my fucking life?

When Alex arrived home I fixed us both a drink. Might as well go out with a bang.

He was noticeably upset that I was drinking again, but he didn't say a word. I waited till we were both seated before I sprang my big news on him. He was understanding and supportive as usual. When I finally told him about the cutting he was mortified. He knew about secret cutting, of course. He'd dealt with clients who cut, but he was stunned to learn I'd been doing it. I think, too, that he felt guilty somehow because he hadn't noticed.

"So," I asked. "Do you think I should go?"

"Yes, sweetheart, I'm afraid so. What do you think?"

"I don't want to." The tears began to fall again.

"I'm sure you don't, but I just don't see another solution right now. Do you?"

"No, I guess not."

"When do you check in?"

"Not till Monday morning. I've got a few things around here I need to get done first."

"What about A Woman's Place? Are you going to attend group?"

"I guess so. I don't know."

"You know, hon, I've always thought you needed to be in a support group for abuse victims. I really think it's important for you to follow through with that also."

"I guess you're right. I'll call them when I get out of rehab." I grimaced. "Yuck. That sounds horrible."

"I'll tell you what, I'll cancel my Monday morning appointments so I can go with you to check in."

"Would you? I'd really appreciate it." I stood up and sat in his lap, my head on his shoulder, tears falling onto his soft, blue shirt. "Oh, Alex, I'm so scared."

"I know, sweetheart. I know." He rubbed my back. "It's the best thing, though. You'll see."

I lay in bed Sunday night, tossing and turning for ages it seemed. I finally got up, made myself a drink, rolled a joint and logged on to the Internet. I figured I wasn't going to get any sleep anyway so I might as well enjoy my last night of freedom. I went to bed at 4:00 a.m., tears rolling down my cheeks.

I struggled to keep my emotions in check Monday morning when I walked into Whispering Pines and up to the receptionist's desk.

"May I help you?" she asked.

"Yes, hi. I'm Ali Connery. I'm here to check in."

"Do you know which unit?"

"Yes, Unit Five. Chemical Dependency."

END

Printed in the United States
4269

9 781588 512987